HARBOTTLE, Philip

Meredith's justice

Meredith's Justice

Raiders who seem intent on destroying every ranch in the valley are terrorizing the district of Mountain Peak in Arizona. When rancher David Meredith becomes their latest victim, it opens a new chapter in the violent and bloody history of the town of Mountain Peak.

Caught up in the maelstrom of events is David's troubled younger brother, Bart Meredith. He is aided – and sometimes led – by his heavyweight father, who shows an amazing talent for ingenious stratagems, and Jane Talbot, a courageous young woman who herself becomes a target for the terrorists.

Can the unlikely team of father and son avenge David Meredith and unmask his killer, or will they join him in death?

Meredith's Justice

PHILIP HARBOTTLE

A Black Horse Western

ROBERT HALE · LONDON

For Matt and Nini Japp

Typeset by
Derek Doyle & Associates, Liverpool.
Printed and bound in Great Britain by
Antony Rowe Limited, Wiltshire

1

DEATH AT THE RANCH

The young woman boarding the train appeared surprisingly cool and serene, considering the still-torrid blaze of the late afternoon sun and the stuffiness of the train. A wealth of blonde hair showed beneath her hat, and her summery frock was unusually stylish for such a region.

Suitcase in hand, she murmured excuses as she eased her way amidst the men and women who had gathered in the corridor, the better to feel the breeze sweeping through the open window as the train resumed its journey into the heart of Arizona.

She hesitated as she came to a compartment with only two men in it. Studying them through the glass she decided they looked a better bet than the average cattle dealer and cowpuncher. One of the men was huge, with a large paunch expanding before him, a black Homburg hat perched four-square on his head. He was dressed entirely in black, against which his collar sharply contrasted.

His younger companion was wedged in the corner seat and apparently snoozing. He was of more normal proportions, though still large limbed. From the cut of his clothes he was plainly not a resident of a hick town; possibly he might be an inhabitant of a city. On the seat beside him lay a second large-brimmed black Homburg.

Satisfied with her survey the girl pushed open the door, and then quickly closed it again as a powerful draught hurtled momentarily through the open carriage window. Turning, she began the job of heaving her suitcase on to the rack.

'Allow me, miss . . .'

'Pardon?' She glanced round. The larger man was looming beside her and giving her a sense of extreme smallness. He had removed his hat to reveal a semi-bald head with grey hair thinning over his ears. His face was round, triple-chinned, with a full-lipped mouth. He was perhaps sixty and, except for his enormous middle, carried himself well.

'At your service, miss,' he murmured, with a slight inclination of his head, and taking the suitcase heaved it up to the rack.

'Thank you,' the girl said, surprised to find courtesy in this region. She settled in the corner seat opposite the dozing young man, then again looked at his companion.

'My name, miss, if you will forgive the liberty, is Meredith,' the Goliath explained. 'Randle Meredith. I am a widower, and this is my son, Bart . . .' He motioned to the sleeping man and made a sound suspiciously like a regretful sigh.

'I'm sorry . . . I mean, I'm pleased to meet you.'

The girl looked out of the window upon the speeding desert wastes and scrubland – and, far away, a backdrop of purple where mountains loomed. Then she looked back at where the enormous Meredith had reseated himself, his hat still discreetly removed.

'Are you by any chance related to the rancher David Meredith?' she asked.

Before Meredith could reply the young man in the corner stirred suddenly and stretched his arms. His eyes opened lazily and looked straight into the steady blue ones of the girl watching him. He deliberately hesitated in his movements, absorbing details. She was young, he decided. Slender, too, with the trimmest legs and neatest figure he had seen for a long time. Not a trace of make-up marred her features. While lacking stunning beauty she had a definite prettiness. There was an air of the outdoors about her, of strength and alertness.

'Hot, isn't it,' Bart Meredith remarked languidly.

'It certainly is, son,' his father agreed – and the young man glanced at him.

'As a matter of fact, Dad, I wasn't addressing you,' he said candidly. Bart returned his attention to the girl, and though she quite realized his remark had been directed at her she made no response. As he had assessed her, so she now assessed him. He was handsome after a fashion, black-haired, with dark-blue eyes. In his late twenties, perhaps. Yet there was something odd about him. Though strength lay in the line of the jaw and set of the mouth, there was a dissolute weakness in his expression, as though he were ill, or . . . something.

'I don't expect to look my best at well over a hundred in the shade,' he told the girl drily, and stretched out long, immaculately suited legs.

She still made no answer, studying him, and decided that when standing he was probably fairly tall.

'The young lady was just asking, son, if we are related to David Meredith,' Meredith remarked, smiling.

'Yes; I heard her.' The young man straightened up and smiled indolently. 'Dave Meredith's my brother,' he explained, and he saw the girl give a little start.

'Oh, is he?' She sat back, clearly surprised. Then, recovering herself, she continued: 'I know David Meredith quite well. He lives only a couple of miles from our ranch – where I live with my stepfather. We have the Slanting F, you know.'

'Have you?' Bart's grin widened. 'These Western terms all sound slightly crazy to me. I'm a city man.'

'I can tell that,' the girl said, and there seemed to be a slight edge of contempt in her voice. 'Which city?'

'Best city there is, far as I'm concerned . . . Boston.'

'You're an Easterner, then?'

'Uh-huh. And I'm not apologizing for it, either.'

The girl reflected. 'I'd always assumed David Meredith had been born in Arizona, same as the rest of us. He was in Mountain Peak Valley when my stepfather started his spread there – and that's fifteen years ago. Since I was only five then I don't remember much about it.'

Bart smiled to himself at this subtle method of revealing her age; then he said:

'My brother is twelve years older than I am, Miss – er—'

'My name's Jane Talbot,' the girl said frankly, and the two men nodded.

'Obviously,' Bart said, extending a gold cigarette-case at which the girl shook her head, 'you're not particularly keen on city men.'

'City men are usually soft.' The girl shrugged. 'And men who are soft don't survive the rigours out here for long.'

A look of bitterness seemed to settle on the dissolute mouth as Bart lighted his cigarette.

'I suppose it kills some and cures others,' he said,

waving the lighted match into extinction. 'Far as I'm concerned I hope it cures.'

'Why? Are you ill?'

'No,' the young man responded, grinning. 'But just the same my father seems to think that it would improve my health no end if we came out here and lived with my brother for an indefinite period. On top of that my old man has the idea that it might make me less irresponsible. Seems a bit late to start, considering I'm twenty-seven, that is . . . Ill? No!' he emphasized. 'You may not think it, but I once was champion wrestler of my college – Judo expert and all the rest of it. Dad here will confirm that.'

'Quite correct, miss,' Meredith verified.

'In other words, the change from Boston to Arizona is supposed to make a man of you?' the girl asked.

'I'm not sure I like the way that you say "supposed".'

'I'm sorry, but you just don't seem like . . . good material,' the girl explained frankly. 'The men out here are as hard as rocks. They have to be to stand it. I find it difficult to believe you are David Meredith's brother. He's about one of the toughest men in Mountain Peak Valley.'

'Once he was a city man, like me,' Bart said. 'The only difference between us is that he left home twenty years ago to live in Arizona from choice; I've come because I've effectively been ordered to. And what I have seen of the West so far I don't like one bit.'

Abruptly the girl got to her feet, her cheeks colouring. Swinging away from him she began to struggle with her suitcase on the rack.

'Hey, just a minute!' Bart jumped up and stumbled over to her as the train rocked. 'I was just talking about the district – the West generally. Nothing personal!'

'I'd like my suitcase,' she said. 'Or are you too city-soft to lift it down?'

Bart did as she asked and gave the suitcase to her. She took it, then left the compartment, closing the door sharply behind her. Bart hesitated over following, sighed, and then returned to his seat in the corner. After a moment or two his father looked at him out of the tail of his eye.

'Can't say I altogether blame the young woman,' he commented drily.

'Be hanged to her,' Bart growled. 'Seems to me that women are all alike – even out here in the West. Can't trust 'em. Turn their noses up at the least thing.'

'A somewhat biased viewpoint, son. Your late mother and I were very happy.'

'I'm sorry, Dad. I didn't mean—'

'I know you didn't, son,' Meredith said quietly. 'I was just thinking that since she resides in the valley where we are heading – Mountain Peak – she might have been invaluable to us in directing the way. I understand that these Western districts are rugged, to say the least of it.'

'We don't need her. Dave will be there with his wagon, or whatever he calls it. Only thing is, the journey might have been less boring with her to talk to . . . Oh, forget her!'

Meredith smiled to himself, aware of the lack of conviction in Bart's voice. Jane Talbot had been different, very different indeed from the socialites with whom Bart had wasted so many hours of his life since reaching manhood.

When the train finally pulled into Mountain Peak it was some six hours late, thanks to the roundabout nature of the route and occasional cattle hold-ups. It was also early morning, which served to make the wayside halt so dead that it was a wonder it was on the map at all.

Bart was not in the best of tempers either. When the train had been held up some ten miles out of Mountain Peak he had watched many of the passengers alight, presumably to find other means of transport to town. Amongst them had been Jane Talbot. Though he insisted he was not in the least interested in her he found that he still had the memory of her slim form striding away into the twilight. And now . . .

He and his father surveyed the dead stillness of the Arizonan railway station at one in the morning and watched the train's rear light vanishing round a bend in the line.

'A dump, Dad – a dump,' Bart commented, putting down his suitcase on the gravelly stones which marked the platform. 'Maybe we should have got off the train when Miss Talbot did.'

'I'm inclined to agree, son,' Meredith said, and turning slowly as though on an invisible turntable he absorbed the view.

The night was coldly bright. The lingering warmth of day had long since radiated into the cloudless sky. The stars looked about ready to fall out of the violet heaven, paling a little to the east where loomed the mighty Catalinas. To the west was a flat, indefinable wilderness cloaked in mist – pastureland, desert, and mesa interwoven in a common grey patchwork, which to the two uninitiated men, told nothing. To north and south the view had the same grey uniformity, except that the dim shapes of huddled buildings – the ramshackle town of Mountain Peak itself – broke the monotony.

Nowhere a light, a movement, or a sound, save a faintly clanging bell echoing from the distance where the train was continuing on its way to Caradoc City.

Bart stirred himself as he sat on the suitcase.

'Thanks to the blasted train getting held up we're hours late and Dave must have gone back to his ranch. What the blazes do we do next?'

Meredith pointed to his right.

'Some kind of dwelling over there. Probably belongs to whoever looks after this station. We can see, anyway.'

He picked up the suitcase and followed Bart to a low-roofed brick outhouse standing at the end of the gravel-stoned platform. It had one window, tightly shut and dark, and a door. Upon it Bart rapped sharply.

There was a long pause, then abruptly the door opened and a shadowy white face appeared.

'Well? What in blue tarnation d'yuh want at this hour o' night?'

'Sorry, but we're strangers around here,' Bart apologized. 'I'm Bart Meredith and this is my father. Where can we get transport? We've got to reach my brother's ranch – the Double Y – in Mountain Peak Valley.'

Long pause, then: 'Say, I reckon you must be Dave Meredith's brother!'

'Right! How do we . . . ?'

'Ain't no horses or buckboards at this hour. Durin' the daytime mebbe, but this is night. So I reckon you'd best walk. Ain't far. About three miles – the Double Y is down the trail apiece. Y'can't miss it. The trail joins the high street.'

'The what?' Meredith inquired.

'High street. I reckon you two jiggers are 'bout six hours late,' he added. 'Your brother Dave were over here durin' the evemn' a-waitin' for yuh. Then he gave up and went back to his spread.'

Abruptly the door closed and the silence of the cemetery descended once more.

'Well, that seems to be that,' Meredith said. 'Presumably we go down the trail apiece.'

His enormous figure moved in the starlight, suitcase in hand, and Bart mooched after him. Together they headed down the cindery road which crunched under their feet, moving towards a handful of wooden buildings.

'I don't think I'm going to like this place one bit,' Bart declared presently.

'I don't know.' Meredith seemed quite philosophic. 'I admit that it appears a trifle dull after Boston, but there is the compensation of these open spaces, the smell of the desert, the sparkling air, the natural life. It may serve your health a lot better than crawling round the city in search of new pleasures.'

Bart did not answer. He and his father might have been the only people in the universe as they walked slowly down the centre of the 'high street', glancing about them as they went. The rising moon only served to accentuate the shoddy flimsiness of the 'town' of Mountain Peak.

The high street was a rutted, sun-baked trail leading between two parallel, railed boardwalks, set back from which were wooden buildings of various sizes. Dimly, signs on windows, or hanging lopsidedly into the street, proclaimed an assayer's, trading store, a drugstore, a livery stable, a lawyer's and sheriff's offices, and – separately, as though respectively proud of their vice and sanctity – the Painted Lady saloon and a tin tabernacle.

'Perhaps this ghost town will assume an air of life when daylight comes,' Meredith commented.

'It needs it! As it is I'd sooner walk through a cemetery and know the folks in it are dead.'

They walked up the high street without anything disturbing the impression of a mausoleum, and found themselves following a broad, rutted wagon-track. Still with the feeling that they were alone in the universe they plodded onwards. Both of them could smell the intangible wind blowing from the desert and mesa, bringing with it its queer suggestion of vast, untamed spaces, of distances reaching out beyond imagination. They listened ever and again to the remote sound of a mountain lion, or the nearer hoot of an owl. Occasionally, startling in its gentleness, wings brushed their faces as a night bird fled before them.

'The West has quite a distinctive atmosphere, don't you think?' Meredith remarked after they had walked perhaps a mile.

'I'd swap the whole lot this moment for a brandy and soda at my club back in Boston! I'm not cut out for this Wild West stuff, Dad. You'll see: it won't cure me. I'll – what was that?' Bart broke off, startled, as something shot across his feet.

'Possibly a pack-rat or a ground squirrel, son. Unless, perhaps it was a figment of – hmm . . .'

'Drink?' Bart suggested. 'OK, say it. I don't mind . . . Oh, for the love of Mike, let's get on to Dave's ranch!'

At the end of two hours' solid tramping there was still no sign of the Double Y ranch and the trail, hard and clear in the rising moonlight, seemed to stretch to infinity. To either side of the trail reared tall, coarse-grass banks topped with small juniper, cedar, and oak trees, their half-developed leaves rustling in the cold wind sweeping down from the mountain heights.

'I think the trees are beginning to thin out,' Meredith said, straining his eyes in the moonlight. 'It looks as though we are coming to pastureland and that should mean ranches.'

He was right. Another half-mile's progress brought the end of the trail where it lost itself in the verdure of a valley.

The rutted, sun-baked dust had changed to a dark carpet of grass. Perched at various angles on the valley's sides were vaguely discernible dwellings, all of them dark as though nobody lived in them.

'Perhaps a dozen or more ranches,' Meredith said, coming to a halt and surveying the scene.

'Out of which we require just one,' Bart reminded him. 'And not one with a light! Dammit, what's Dave playing at? He could have left a lighted window as a guide for us turning up late – or something.'

'He might – unless he has given up expecting us until tomorrow. Only thing we can do is to conduct a search of these ranches to discover the right one . . .'

The going was easier on the springy grass and ten minutes brought them to the first of the ranches. Over the main gateway it said – SLANTING F.

'Mmm. Jane Talbot's place,' Bart murmured. 'And I suppose she's hit the hay like the rest of 'em . . . What else is there?'

The two men went further and examined several more ranches, marvelling inwardly at the various designations they discovered, before they arrived at a fairly large-sized spread with a double Y carved out of wood perched over the open yard gates.

' 'Bout time,' Bart commented, studying the dark mass of the ranch house and the extensive corrals. 'No red carpet out,' he added drily.

'Or any cattle in the corrals,' Meredith mused, and there was anxiety in his tone. 'The further corral gates are open, and there aren't any cattle anywhere.'

'Meaning rustlers?' Bart suggested drily. 'You've been reading too many dime novels, Dad. If there are no steers in the corral I'm pretty sure Dave knows what he's about.'

Meredith in the lead they crossed the deserted yard,

passing a solitary buckboard outside the stables, and so reached the three steps leading to the ranch house porch. The outer screen door was closed and, so it appeared in the dim light, was the main door behind it. Meredith knocked discreetly and then waited.

'You're too gentle, Dad,' Bart told him, and kicked his heel violently on the frame. Then, to his surprise, the screen door vibrated and swung slightly to and fro.

'Open!' Meredith exclaimed. 'I don't like this, son.'

Puzzled that his brother should leave the door undone – unless it were left that way on purpose so Bart and his father could enter – Bart tugged the screen door wide and found the inner door also unlocked. He entered a dark stretch of what he judged to be a hall, his father coming up in the rear and blocking the vague moonlight with his huge figure.

'Hello there, Dave!' Bart called. 'You anywhere about?'

The ranch house remained dark and undisturbed.

'Fine welcome this is,' Bart muttered. Finding his matches, he struck one and in the splutter of yellow flame held high over his head he and his father peered about them. As they had judged, they were in a hall. From it led four doors, one of them open. Automatically they moved towards it, but the match-flame expired before they reached it.

'More I see of this the less I understand it,' Bart said, as a match-head scraped again. 'Dave seems to have – *My God*!'

Both men both dropped their suitcases, their fingers giving way in sheer surprise. Together they stared blankly at a long-legged figure in riding-pants and check shirt swinging six feet from the wooden floor, a strong rope knotted about his neck and carried over a central overhead beam.

'He's . . .' The words stuck in Bart's throat and the match went out as it scorched his fingers. Recovering himself Meredith dived forward in the gloom and grasped the body, raising it so that the weight was taken from the rope.

'Still warm,' he said, breathing hard. 'But I'm afraid he's dead. Quick – we need another light. Find a lamp or something.'

Another lighted match in his hand Bart stumbled about amidst the furniture, then a dim yellow glow began to cast upon the fairly comfortable living-room, log-walled, the niches plugged with red clay. There were rough but serviceable chairs, a bureau, an old-fashioned safe, a table, and matting and skin rugs were on various parts of the floor.

'I'm cutting him down,' Meredith said. 'He's a dead weight.'

Bart had to force himself to look at the swinging body: the staring eyes, protruding tongue, and blue-white complexion . . . then he gave his father a hand and between them they lowered the body reverently to the floor.

'It's Dave all right,' Bart muttered, staring down at the face.

'Yes, son. A trifle older than I remember him from ten years ago when he came to your mother's funeral . . .' He paused, struggling to find words. 'Thank God she never lived to see . . . *this*.'

'Why did it happen, Dad? What terrible thing could have led him to take his own life?'

'Don't talk like a fool!' Meredith snapped. 'David was *murdered*! Look around you – there is no article of furniture nearby from which he could have jumped. The length of rope is only a couple of feet and the nearest

17

furniture is yards away . . .'

'God, you're right, Dad,' Bart whispered. 'He must have been lifted to the beam and hanged from it.'

The logic had an inescapable quality, and it deepened Bart's frown.

'But who'd *want* to kill him? Last I heard from him he said he was doing fine here – and prospering.'

'If he were prospering, son, there would have been cattle in the corral. I was uneasy about that and now I'm afraid we have the explanation. The open gates suggest that the cattle have been driven elsewhere, and as for poor David – his fate is obvious.'

'What do we do in a case like this?' Bart gave an uneasy glance about him. 'Advise the sheriff?'

'We'll have to, but frankly, son . . .' Meredith put his hand to his eyes, 'Right now, I can't face another journey back to town on foot. I just don't seem to have the strength . . .'

'Of course, Dad.' Bart moved forward and put his arms around his father's shoulders. 'Dave can't be any deader in the morning than he is now so we'll leave it till then and try and get some rest. Better find yourself a chair whilst I carry Dave's body into a bedroom.'

Meredith slumped into the nearest chair. The immediate horror of the discovery was fading, to be replaced by a smouldering anger and resolve to find the man – or men – responsible for his elder son's murder.

Bart meanwhile had located the nearest bedroom, and laid the corpse gently on to the bed and then covered it with a rug. He stood with head bowed for perhaps a minute, then, coming to himself, he went in search of the kitchen.

In ten minutes baked beans, some toast and coffee were on the rough table and the two men settled down. The lamplight illuminated their tired, travel-and-grief-stained faces. Bart's dark-blue eyes were puzzled, even a little afraid, as he ate and reflected.

His father, on the other hand, was increasingly looking as if he had – outwardly at least – completely come to terms with the unexpected tragedy they had found. It was almost as if the transference from their comfortable city atmosphere of the Meredith residence in Boston to this rustic backwoods of the world had given him a new purpose and challenge in life. One he intended to meet head-on.

Presently Bart asked a question:

'Do you suppose it would do any good if we asked the other ranchers whether they've any notions about what's happened?'

Meredith considered as he drank his coffee, then he shook his semi-bald head.

'They might resent being awakened at this hour of the night to be asked a lot of difficult questions. We're Easterners, don't forget, and that might breed hostility from the locals – as Miss Talbot made evident. I think we should leave things alone until the morning and then inform the sheriff. We should at least be able to borrow horses from a neighbouring ranch to make the journey into town.'

'Granting I can remember how to ride one,' Bart said. 'It's years since I was taught by Dave how to do it. Don't like the beasts . . .' Bart struggled to muffle a yawn behind his hand and then glanced at his watch. 'Hell, it's four o'clock! I noticed earlier that there are two beds in the room over there, Dad.' He nodded in its direction. 'Dave must have prepared them for us, before . . . before . . .'

'He was murdered,' Meredith finished, heaving himself

19

slowly to his feet. 'OK son, let's turn in, and try and get what rest we can.'

2

FUNERAL PYRE

Meredith opened his eyes, absorbing the moonlit home-
spun details of the rustic bedroom. He felt sure that he
had heard something other than the deep breathing of
Bart lying flat out, fully dressed – except for collar and tie
– beside him. His uncertainty was banished when there
came out of the silence the sudden movement of heavy
feet in the adjoining living-room, and then the muttering
of voices.

Meredith nudged Bart gently and then put a hand over
his mouth to stifle any remarks he might make.

'Intruders, son,' Meredith murmured. 'In the living-
room. We'd best check – but quietly!'

He rolled his gross bulk from the bed and padded in
bare feet to the closed door. Stooping, he peered through
the keyhole. In the room beyond the oil-lamp had been
lighted and made dimly visible three figures as they
conversed in low tones. One was holding a wad of green-
backed dollars, about which an argument seemed to be in
progress.

'Outlaws,' Meredith whispered, moving aside to allow Bart to look. 'They seem to be robbing the safe.'

'All of them with kerchiefs to their eyes,' Bart muttered. 'That doesn't help us much . . .'

'The man doing most of the talking has a rather interesting gun belt,' Meredith commented. 'The one with the left-hand gun in it.'

Bart peered again. 'Yes – I see what you mean. The end of it is broken off. Maybe that will make it identifiable later on. What do we do now?' He glanced up. 'They could be Dave's killers, but we can't risk tackling them unarmed . . .'

'Perhaps there's a gun somewhere in this room,' Meredith said, and turned aside to search in the rough wooden dressing-table. Unfortunately he searched too thoroughly and in the dark the top drawer shot out of the wooden slots and crashed to the floor.

Instantly the bedroom door flew open and a masked gunman stood there, dimly visible in the moonlight, with twin guns levelled.

'Say, fellers,' he called back into the living-room, 'I reckon we don't need to wonder no more who cut the stiff down. Just as well we came back to see what there was in the safe!'

'Yeah,' another commented. 'Though I still says we should ha' looked the first time.'

Three other men came in, one of them the man with the broken-ended gun belt. Silently they contemplated the enormous Meredith and then Bart as he hovered near the bed wondering what to do.

'Well, boss?' asked the man with the guns. 'Do we dry-gulch these critters?'

'First I'd like to know who these guys are,' Broken Belt responded, and it was obvious he was disguising his voice.

'Give – both of you!' he ordered. 'You a couple of saddle tramps, or what?'

'It's you who should be answering questions,' Bart snapped. 'Which one of you murdered my brother?'

'Brother!' exclaimed Broken Belt. 'A tenderfoot like you? And who's this with the belly?'

'I'm his father – and father of the man you killed,' Meredith answered with dignity, and icy control. 'Why did you murder him?'

'He was a good-for-nothin' louse!' Broken Belt snapped. 'And it struck me later we might as well come back and see what he'd got in his safe. From the looks of his breed you ain't much better, neither. OK, boys, hand it to 'em,' he finished briefly.

The guns became steady, and Meredith sprang. He had no exact idea what he intended doing except that it was clearly imperative he deflect the aim of the nearest gunman. Weighing some seventeen stone plus and moving at high speed he sent the man hurtling backwards before a well-aimed and savage blow in the stomach. There was the crash of a chair as the man fell into it and it broke under the impact.

Knowing it probably meant his death if he did not act, Bart flung himself forward too. It seemed that something exploded in his face and he found himself flying back across the bed, to crash helplessly on the floor on the other side. A revolver blazed and a bullet whanged into the wooden wall close to his face.

Meredith slewed round like a whipped elephant in the darkness and tripped over the troublesome drawer. He whipped it up, whirled it round and released it as a gun blazed at him. By a fraction the bullet missed and split a mirror in a tinkle of exploding shards. Not a second later the heavy drawer struck Broken Belt under the chin and

23

sent him keeling backwards through the doorway. He struck the table in the living-room, made a grab at it to save himself, and knocked over the oil-lamp. Instantly the flame gushed up from the spilled spirit.

Magically the gunmen called off the attack. Fully aware of the danger from the bone-dry timber of the ranch they floundered through the living-room and out on to the porch. Meredith stared blankly for a moment at the savagely spreading flame – then he hurried round to Bart and dragged him to his feet.

Still dazed, Bart found himself hoisted with a 'fireman's lift'. His father lurched with him to the nearest window.

'Quickly, son!' he gasped, swinging Bart about so that his feet faced the window. 'Kick the glass out!'

Instinctively Bart lashed out, and kicked out the glass. Meredith unceremoniously heaved Bart outside, before scrambling through after him. He caught his arm as he swayed dizzily, still barely recovered from the knockout, and they drew away from the already blazing ranch house. The rapidity of the fire's progress possibly explained the anxiety of the gunmen to escape.

In five minutes the entire ranch was a crackling, scorching inferno, the sparks igniting the stables and distant bunkhouse, which in turn added their flames to the blaze.

'Dave's cremation, I'm afraid,' Bart murmured, recovered now and studying the holocaust in sombre awe.

Meredith did not answer, grimly watching the funeral pyre of his elder son.

So absorbed were they in watching the ranch burn they failed to notice a gathering of horses and riders some distance behind them as the occupants of the neighbouring ranches came out to investigate the events. Then, turning as the fire began to die down, Meredith caught sight of the other spectators.

He decided there were a couple of dozen men and women present, leaning on their saddle horns and watching. Then one man jogged his horse forward and became visible as a broad-shouldered individual in a black Stetson, a mackinaw drawn over his check shirt in the chilly morning air.

'What gives?' he inquired briefly.

'Gunmen,' Bart responded. 'They murdered my brother by hanging him – and then they accidentally burned down the ranch . . .' He added the details and the man on the impatient horse nodded slowly when the story was finished.

'Same gang again, I reckon,' he growled, 'and they had the gall to come back and open the safe. I'm Sheriff Curtis. One of my deputies on night duty saw the fire from the town yonder and told me about it, so I came over to take a look. It wasn't fear of fire that drove those hoodlums away,' he added. 'They knew I'd be here with my deputies mighty quick once the flames were seen.'

'Pity you weren't here before my brother got murdered,' Bart commented bitterly.

'It isn't Mr Curtis's fault,' a woman's voice said firmly, and Bart turned to look at another rider who had just come up. In the combined light of the fire and moon he could see that she had loose fair hair and, as far as he could judge, a reasonably pretty face and young figure.

'Well, if it isn't Miss Talbot!' he remarked drily. 'And apparently still determined to pick on me! And how do you know it isn't the sheriff's fault?'

'We all know it. One man and a couple of deputies can't hope to control or even keep track of the crimes that happen in this valley. In the past few months there have been numerous onslaughts – and with them about six murders and destroyed spreads.'

25

'Then that's a damned disgrace!' Bart declared. 'How can all of you possibly allow such things?'

'Ain't a question of allowin' it,' one man commented. 'We just can't stop it! They ain't renamed this territory "Death Valley" for nothin'.'

'Being new here, I guess you don't know how things stand,' the sheriff said quietly. 'Ordinarily, I'd have to question you and your father about this murder – but I just don't need to do that. You say it was gunmen and I know you're right. There's nothin' we can do about it: we're up against organized terror which none of us has yet had a chance to break.'

'OK, I'm too tired to argue about it any more,' Bart sighed. 'My father and I now have no roof over our heads. Is there a hotel in this cock-eyed dump?'

'Sure there is,' Curtis responded. 'There's the Mountain Hotel back in town – or there's Ma Doyle's roomin'-house. If somebody can loan you a couple of horses, I'll take you back with me and fix things up—'

'There's no need for that, Sheriff,' Jane Talbot interrupted. 'Mr Meredith and his son can stay with my stepfather and me at our place, the Slanting F.'

The girl slid from her mount and revealed that she was wearing riding-pants, half-boots, check shirt, and a leather jacket. Bart found her nearness profoundly disturbing – even more so after his stolid declarations that he had shut her right out of his mind.

'You sure about that?' he demanded. 'After the way you bawled me out on the train . . .'

'Oh, forget that!' she interrupted. 'Maybe I was edgy with the heat – maybe lots of things. In this region there's a sort of code amongst us that if a neighbour gets in a spot those more fortunate should help him out of it.'

'Sounds like a nice code,' Meredith commented, smiling in the dim light. 'We'd be delighted to accept your offer, Miss Talbot.'

'In the morning, I'll organize a party to try and find the cattle. No use us lookin' for them in the dark.' With that, Curtis turned and nudged his horse away.

Gradually the spectators dissolved into the grey dimness of approaching dawn. The smoking embers of the Double Y glowed red briefly as the cool wind presaging the daylight stirred them and then dropped again.

'We'll have to walk to my place,' Jane said. 'I've only my little pinto here . . .' She nodded to the small horse whose reins she was holding.

On an impulse, Bart took the girl's arm and they began walking. He smiled as she made no attempt to pull herself free. There came upon him again that same odd feeling of being alone with her in the universe – except for the very earthy clumping of his father, walking discreetly in the background. There was something unfathomable about this spaciousness – a sense of immense grandeur, of boundless freedom for the soul.

'You know,' the girl murmured, as the pinto's bridle clinked gently, 'it seems odd that you and your father should have come out West. Don't you think you ought to explain why you are really here? You father says you're not ill, so what can be wrong with you?'

'It's not a particularly pretty or interesting story,' Bart said slowly as they walked along in the perceptibly strengthening light. 'Simply told, Miss Talbot, I'm a waster.'

'That's no surprise,' the girl said. 'Candidly, I gathered when I first set eyes on you that you hadn't lived a particularly . . . well, *healthy* life. You've got the frame and features of a real man, but you've let both of them go to seed. What was it?' she asked calmly. 'Drink?'

'Uh-huh,' Bart admitted, 'and moneyed women, with nothing better to do but hang around and make themselves nuisances. In all honesty I didn't really want to be bothered with them. I just couldn't help myself . . .'

'Your father told me he was a widower,' the girl said gently. 'That have anything to do with things?'

'Indirectly . . .' Bart hesitated, then, deciding that the girl was genuinely interested, he continued his story. 'My brother Dave was twelve years older than me, and he decided that he didn't want to go into my father's business in Boston. So when he was eighteen, he left home, and headed out West to make his own way as a cowboy. Eventually, as you know, he became a rancher here in Mountain Valley. I was only six when he left, of course, so I stayed behind with my parents in Boston. I guess they rather spoiled me, especially my mother—'

'Hardly surprising, son, was it, with David gone?' Bart gave a little start, and twirled round to look at his father, who had been listening intently. He gave a somewhat embarrassed smile.

'Sorry, Dad. You don't mind me talking like this, do you? Miss Talbot was asking, and—'

'I know – I heard. Go right ahead.'

'When Mother caught a fever and died unexpectedly about ten years ago, I guess I started drinking a little more than was good for me. My mother's will had settled a pretty generous allowance on me, so I didn't really need to work, and had no particular occupation. So I became easy prey. Eventually the old man put his foot down and told me to become a man . . . or else, as you say out here. The way things are going,' Bart finished moodily, 'I'm afraid it's going to be "or else".'

'From which I gather you still don't like the West?'

'No I don't like the West much,' Bart confessed. 'Hardly

to be expected when I'm used to Boston. Only the way things have turned out – the brutal murder of my brother, for instance – makes me think pretty hard. Frankly I feel like running for it.'

'And are you going to?' Jane asked in quiet contempt.

'No. I think I'll stay around for a while and see if I can find out anything that might lead me to my brother's murderer. It'll be tough going for a lily-white like me but I'll try it.'

'I'm glad to hear you say that, son,' Meredith said quietly. 'I'd already made up my mind to stay here, to try and avenge David's death – with or without your help.'

'And I'll help you, as well,' Jane said, in her matter-of-fact voice; then the conversation lapsed as they came to the big open double gates of the Slanting F. The girl led the way across the wide expanse of yard, put her horse in the stables, and then went up the three steps to the porch.

She pulled open the screen door, motioned the men to follow, and led the way across a wide wooden-walled hall and then into a big living-room. The curtains were not drawn and the waxing grey of daylight was cast upon comfortable furniture, a huge stone fireplace, costly skin rugs, and the latest pattern in oil-lamps. In fact the impression conveyed was one of money.

'Just make yourselves comfortable,' she invited, with a little motion of her hand. 'I'd better tell my stepfather that you're here—'

'Won't be any need for that, I reckon,' a voice commented, and a tall, rangy man of late middle age came into the room. From the tousled look of his grey hair he seemed to have been sleeping. He was loosely dressed in a check shirt and heavy grey trousers supported by a wide belt. Bart's eyes strayed almost automatically to the belt, and then away again. There was nothing the matter with it, and in any case it was not a gun belt.

'Oh, here you are, Dad . . .' Jane hurried over to him. 'I was just going to wake you up.'

'I wasn't asleep. I've been watching the rumpus over at the Double Y from my bedroom window – then I saw you come in with these two strangers. What was it this time? Same gang again?'

'Seems so,' Jane said gravely.

'Dad-blamed outlaws,' her stepfather breathed savagely; then he checked himself and smiled ruefully at Bart and Meredith as they stood regarding him. He was a handsome man in every way – hook-nosed, square jawed, with a fierce resolution in his clear blue eyes. Everywhere that exposed skin was revealed it had the deep burned-in brown of the outdoor man.

'This is Mr Randle Meredith, and his son Bart – brother of Dave Meredith,' the girl explained, and a look of surprise crossed her stepfather's face.

'Say, that's good hearing in one sense, Mr Meredith – but durned bad in another. It was your son's ranch which went up in smoke, wasn't it?'

'And his dead body with it,' Meredith replied grimly, his hand vanishing in the grip of the steel fingers.

'Dead? Dave?' The big Westerner stared incredulously.

'We'll tell you about it, Dad,' Jane said practically, then added: 'To finish the introduction, gentlemen, this is my stepfather, Mr Farnon.'

'Mike Farnon to you gents,' Farnon said, grinning. 'Don't stand on formality, I reckon . . . What brings you into this region, anyways? You don't look the type to me, either of you.'

Jane said quickly: 'Bart is here for his health. He found

that city life wasn't doing him any good and his doctor ordered sunshine. So he came out here with his father, to join his brother, and found him dead. I . . . I met them earlier, on the train, on my way back from seeing my cousin Barbara.'

'Oh, you did?' Farnon remarked, with a leathery grin.

'Then later I saw the fire and rushed out to have a look. Knowing they were headed for that ranch I'd more than a normal interest. I told them they could stay here until they've decided what to do. So there it is, Dad. Dave Meredith has met the same fate as has been dealt out to quite a lot of other settlers in this valley.'

'Yeah, the same fate,' Farnon mused, his brows down; then he shrugged. 'Reckon there's nothing we can do about it right now. There are other things to attend to. You gents will be needin' some rest after all you've been through. And a meal, huh?'

'And a drink,' Bart added. 'Whiskey for preference.'

Meredith cleared his throat gently and looked at the ceiling. Bart glanced at him and then grinned.

'That noise was meant to remind me that I'm supposed to be on the water-wagon,' he explained.

'Why get off it?' Jane asked, in her direct way, and the look of scorn had come back into her blue eyes. 'There's no need for the beastly stuff!'

'That's a woman's way of looking at it,' Farnon said, going over to the sideboard. 'If you want a drink, Bart, you shall have one.'

Bart hesitated, his eyes on Jane's. Then he turned suddenly.

'Forget it, Mr Farnon,' he said briefly. 'If I drink at all it'll be coffee. I don't think I'll bother trying to sleep. I'll freshen up and then perhaps we can have some breakfast. And I want to pay for whatever—'

'No, sir,' Farnon said firmly, shaking his head. 'I'm not that kind of a guy. You can stay as long as you like – and welcome. Now come this way and I'll show you where you and your father can bunk.'

3

SECRET PLAN

'I'd like to know,' Bart said, during breakfast, 'just what is going on in this valley. I'm not a Westerner, of course, but I do know that the day of lawless terrorism ought to have gone by this time.'

'There'll always be terrorism when ruthless gunmen set out on a plan of extermination,' Mike Farnon responded, and Jane gave a quiet nod of confirmation.

Bart said nothing for a moment. He and his father and the girl and her stepfather were seated in the living-room before rashers, eggs, toast and coffee – everything the two men needed to banish the effects of a sleepless night preceded by a wearying journey. But for the fact that they had both slept a good deal in the train they would have been worn out. As it was they were carefully shaved, and with the removal of the shadow from his jaw Bart looked less dissolute than on the day before. The incident of finding his brother murdered and the brush with the gunman had already done something to him.

'What are these gunmen aiming at?' he asked presently. 'It can't just be extermination. Surely there is some *reason* behind it all?'

'There may be,' Mike Farnon said, musing, 'but I'll be darned if I know what it is. Naturally all of us around here have had our heads together tryin' to figure out what these outlaws is aimin' at, but there just doesn't seem to be any sense or reason to it. They come suddenly, by night, shoot the inmates of a spread, turn the cattle loose – not even troublin' to rustle them, which is mighty queer – and then vanishin' the way they came. And not one of us has ever been able to tell who's amongst the gang, and even less who's the head of it.'

'Just shooting for shooting's sake?' Bart asked.

'That's the way it looks to me,' Farnon assented, still scowling. 'It started about a year ago, and it's been goin' on ever since at intervals. The sheriff and his boys, and we ranchers, have all tried to get these critters. We've laid traps, stopped up all night, done everythin' we can to dry-gulch 'em, but every time they seem to know our plans in advance and . . .' Farnon shrugged his big shoulders, 'there it is.'

'It's going to be a tough job trying to find out anything about them,' Bart said reflectively. 'Even tougher to discover which of them was directly responsible for the murder of my brother.'

'You aimin' to do that?' Farnon inquired, raising shaggy eyebrows.

'I may be,' Bart responded, cautiously. 'Naturally, my father and I want the killers brought to justice. So far we've just one clue – one of the men who looked as though he might have been the ringleader of the group was wearing a gun belt with the end broken off, leaving a jagged edge.'

'Reckon you might have something there at that,' Farnon admitted. 'A gun belt is somethin' a man has to wear around here if he's to keep healthy – with hardware in it, of course. If that guy didn't know you saw the gun belt—'

The conversation lapsed as the breakfast continued, then Meredith said: 'I think that in the broken gun belt we have a basis for investigation. All good detectives must have that, of course, and I feel that what the law cannot do, we might.'

Mike Farnon smiled slightly. 'Naturally, I'll help you – so will Jane – wherever we can.' The girl nodded composedly.

'Thanks,' Bart said. 'First of all I think I'll take a look round and see if I can get the feel of this region. At this moment I can still taste Boston and it takes the deuce of a lot of moving.'

'You'll grow to like the West,' Jane said quietly. 'It's something that eventually becomes a part of you, no matter how you may feel at first.'

After breakfast Bart decided on a walk down the valley as far as his late brother's destroyed ranch, having expressed the idea that there might be some clue to be found. Inevitably his father went with him, and in his black suit and Homburg hat there could hardly have been a more incongruous figure in all Arizona.

'This,' he commented, as he and Bart wandered through the charred wood and ashes of the ranch, 'looks like being a waste of time.'

'Maybe it is, but we're getting the fresh air.'

'And the "feel" of things, son?'

Bart came to a stop and turned. 'I said that because there was nothing else I could say,' Bart explained. 'Dammit, Dad, I can talk to you because you understand me. That girl Jane Talbot expects me to go gunning for the men who killed Dave!'

'I thought we'd agreed that's just what we would be doing?'

35

Bart sighed and spread his hands. 'Do I look to you like a tough man of the plains? I've had time to think since last night. I'm just fishing around here to look as though I'm doing something. I don't think I can stand much more of this place.' Brad squinted at the blazing sun and the aridity of the desert beyond the pastureland; then his eyes moved to the looming mountains close by. 'Sorry, Dad – but I'm a city man, not a cowpuncher or glorified Western detective.'

Meredith merely sighed, searched about for and presently found a long stick. With it he began to poke about in the ashes.

'What's the idea, Dad?'

'It occurred to me that if David had been shot we might locate a bullet in the ashes – even from his body if the fire burned him fiercely enough for the bullet to be freed. A ghoulish idea, but it has its possibilities.'

'It's an idea,' Bart agreed. 'What would you do if you found it? Run with it to the sheriff and ask him to—'

'No, we'd retain it, examine it minutely, and maybe at a later date discover the person who owns the gun that fired that particular bullet. We might even draw his fire,' Meredith added, standing with stomach out-thrust and fondling his chins.

Brad shrugged and leaned back against one of the tall mesquite posts supporting the rail around the empty corral. Sudden hoofbeats made him glance up. It was Jane Talbot who came riding into the blazing sunlight, her blonde hair streaming, the scarlet kerchief at her throat flapping in the soft breeze.

'Decided to follow us up?' Bart said, tugging off his hat and smiling.

The girl slid from her horse, a dainty but compact figure in her silk shirt and riding-pants. She tied the reins to the fence before she turned and answered:

'I'm here to help you. You said that you wanted to get the feel of the place – but you won't get far wandering about here without a guide.'

'I'm all yours,' Bart smiled. 'Where do we go first?'

'Into town. You're going to get yourself properly dressed.' Jane folded her arms and smiled. 'Just look at yourself, in your city suit and soft hat! If you're going to start searching for your brother's murderer you've got to dress as do all the men out here – for hard work. They'll take advantage of you in every direction if they think you're a city dude.'

'Miss Jane is right, son. I think we should go with her,' Meredith commented, dropping his stick and strolling over to them. 'Trying to find a bullet here is too much like the proverbial needle in a haystack. Perhaps we'd do better on searching for the man with the broken gun belt.'

'Just a minute, both of you!' Bart held up his hands and looked from one to the other. 'You seem to have taken it for granted that I'm going to look for my brother's murderer. I may have other ideas!'

'You can't have if you're a real man,' Jane stated simply, and Bart stared at her. Ignoring his protesting expression she went on: 'Both of you need proper Western clothes – and guns,' she insisted. 'Especially in this valley where anything can happen. Come back with me to the ranch: there are a couple of horses you can borrow. An extra strong sorrel for you, Mr Meredith,' she added, laughing.

'How well you anticipate my needs, miss,' Meredith said, his smile widening.

'All right then, let's go,' Bart said, but his expression was uneasy as he tramped beside the girl once she had released her horse from the fence.

'Afraid of the men who killed your brother?' she asked gently.

'No!' Bart snapped. 'But it seems to me that in trying to find a murderer – or murderers – amongst a lot of Western cut-throats I shall be committing suicide. What chance will I stand against trained gunmen? I've never even held a gun, let alone fired one.'

'You can learn,' Jane said. 'I can split a manzanita sapling in twain at two hundred feet. I can teach you to do the same thing.'

'Determined to make a tough guy out of me, aren't you.'

'Determined to make you like the West . . . Bart.'

At the mention of his Christian name, Bart paused and looked at the girl steadily. The sun gave her fair hair an entrancing halo.

'That make it all right for me to call you Jane?' he asked.

'Of course. There are no formalities in these parts, Bart.' The girl gave a broad smile. 'We all call each other by our first names.'

Bart could not help but notice how white her teeth were, and how one of her upper front teeth was larger than the others, which gave her smile a roguish quality. Then he became gloomy again, thumbs latched on his trousers pockets as he mooched along at her side. He looked up presently as the superb voice of a grosbeak lifted in the shimmering air. From somewhere came the croaking note of a raven.

'And you say you don't like the West,' Jane murmured, as she caught Bart with his ear cocked to the various sounds.

'I just don't understand it,' he answered defensively.

The girl deliberately stopped him, her slim hand on his arm. She made him look out across the richness of the pastureland to where the yellow and red lichens peeped out from amidst the purple pentstemon at the base of the mountains. She held a finger up to call attention to the mating call of the Sonora pigeon, and the strident cry of a rock-wren as it flew suddenly from a nearby cat-claw bush.

'No man who has any humanity at all can hate this,' Jane insisted. She pointed out beyond the pastureland to the east where the mesa clothed in golden brittle-bush and creamy white yuccas, stretched away to the languorous purple of the horizon.

'Yes . . . it has something,' Bart confessed, as he felt the soft, scented wind upon his face.

'The town's very different,' Jane said, resuming the walk towards the Slanting F with the pinto loping beside her. 'Or maybe you know that already.'

'The town? I saw it in the early hours. Deader than anything I've ever seen. People do live there, then?'

'Mountain Peak is quite a busy place by day – as you'll see.'

Since they had reached the ranch the girl said no more. She gave instructions to the foreman and presently he saddled and brought out two horses – one a slender, well-built mare and the other a broad-backed sorrel. Meredith considered it critically, then without the slightest effort put his foot in the stirrup and swung up into the saddle. Bart stared up at him.

'Where the blazes did you ever learn to mount a horse like that, Dad?'

'The Boston Equine Club, son. In my spare time I enjoyed horse-riding quite a deal, and apparently it is now going to stand me in good stead.'

'Apparently,' Bart agreed, and with the girl's help he struggled up into the saddle of the mare and clung tightly to the horn. 'A long time since I rode a horse – and then I never liked it,' he explained, somewhat embarrassed.

With an agile swing the girl mounted her pinto and led the way out of the yard, Bart jogging behind her uncomfortably with his knees tightly jammed into the mare's sides. Meredith came up behind him with the mellow dignity of a caliph, his Homburg hat set dead square on his round head. After a while, as they struck the trail, he caught up with the girl. He glanced briefly at her waist.

'I do not see you armed, Miss Jane,' he commented. 'Considering the fact that this is a dangerous valley, I'd have thought—'

'But I *am* armed,' she responded, and with a swift movement she flashed her hand inside her shirt and brought it out again, holding a .32 automatic.

'Shoulder holster?' Meredith hazarded.

'That's it. Safest place.'

'Jane, take care what you're doing with that confounded gun!' Bart warned, coming up in the rear. 'The jolting of your horse might cause you to fire accidentally!'

The girl merely smiled, levelled the automatic, sighted, and then fired. Her pinto jumped nervously at the report and some distance away a sapling split in two.

'Nice, but dangerous,' Bart commented worriedly.

Before the girl could return the automatic to the holster Meredith held out his hand.

'If I may, miss—?' Surprised, she gave it to him.

Allowing his sorrel to follow its own course for a moment Meredith took off his Homburg hat with his left hand and tossed it in the air; then with his right he fired, catching the hat as it came down. He beamed as he surveyed the neatly drilled hole through the crown.

'In this region ventilation is very necessary,' he observed. 'And thank you, miss, for the loan of the gun.'

As the girl stared blankly Bart urged his mare forward

and peered at his father as he solemnly put the hat back on his semi-bald head.

'For the love of Pete, Dad, where did you ever learn to shoot like that?'

'I am – or was, when in civilization – rather addicted to funfairs and rifle ranges, son. That is where I learned the gentle art – which, with my ability to sit a horse, may yet serve me well in this valley of no-goods.'

Bart looked at the girl and saw her repressing a laugh. No more was said until the town was reached, and as they rode slowly through the high street Bart looked about him in considerable astonishment, trying to recognize the place as the mausoleum through which he and his father had passed in the early hours.

At this time, mid-morning, it was exceptionally busy. Men and women were going back and forth along the boardwalks, coming in and out of one or other of the stores or offices. In the street itself were those on horseback, several buckboards and teams, with a lone man or woman walking amidst them with a profound unconcern for being suddenly trampled.

Inevitably, as the trio progressed, attention was drawn to the pompous-looking Meredith, bolt upright on his sorrel with his Homburg hat firmly in place – and the uncomfortable-looking young man who was half-fallen in his saddle and clinging to the horn as though it were the spar of a sinking ship. Punchers leaning on the boardwalk hitch rails and smoking grinned at each other and spat contemptuously into the dust. Here and there one or other of them met the cold stare in Jane Talbot's blue eyes and did not make their cynicism quite so obvious.

'Seems to me I'm labelled as a city dude all right,' Bart remarked, glancing about him. 'You were right, Jane.'

'How long they think it depends on you,' she

responded. 'If you behave as roughnecked as they do they'll respect you. If you don't . . .'

'Heaven help you,' Meredith commented; and the girl nodded.

'And amongst all these tough eggs I'm supposed to locate a murderer, or a man with a torn gun belt?' Bart asked. 'I can think of easier jobs.'

The girl did not pursue the topic, but her expression showed quite plainly that she was expecting Bart to behave as any man of the West should.

'Here we are,' Jane said finally, and slid from her horse outside a rambling wooden structure with the uneven legend TOWN STORE across its big window. 'You can get all you need here; that is if you have money.'

'About eight hundred dollars at the moment, which should be more than enough,' Bart said. 'And plenty more in the state bank.' He dismounted gingerly and wondered if he would have to walk bow-legged for the rest of his life.

Meredith stood to one side and the shadow of a grin hovered on his round face as he followed the girl and Bart into the store. A very nasal man in shirt-sleeves and baize apron seemed to gather instantly what the girl meant by an 'outfit', and Bart found himself thrust into a back room supplied with mirrors where he could try on the store's offerings.

At length he emerged again, feeling decidedly embarrassed, and faced the critical eyes of the storekeeper, Jane, and his father. Near them a tall fellow in black with a gambler's shoestring tie depending down his white shirt-front was also looking. He was leaning on an apple barrel, smoking a black cheroot. As Brad appeared he removed the cheroot from his teeth, cuffed up his black Stetson on to his forehead, and then whistled.

'I'll be doggoned!' he commented incredulously.

Bart gave him a sharp look and then came forward into the store. He was feeling uncomfortable, even though his attire was exactly right. Whipcord pants, half-boots with spurs, a check shirt, and a white Stetson. He fingered the purple kerchief at his neck irritably.

'This blasted thing tickles me,' he complained.

'Not what's ticklin' me, I reckon,' the stranger against the apple barrel commented.

He was a tall, well-built man in the mid-thirties, handsome after a fashion, with a Mexican ruggedness of mouth and nose. His complexion was tanned brick-red which stamped him as a native of these sun-drenched wastes. Bart's eyes strayed to the gun belt. It was a single one, and the end was in perfect condition.

'Can't say I've ever met you before,' Bart said at last.

'Nope, guess you haven't. I just came in, ran into Jane, and stayed for a few words – and to have a look at you. Now I've seen everythin'.'

As Bart glared the girl broke in quickly:

'This is Don Saunders, Bart. He owns the Painted Lady saloon down the high street. Don's probably one of the best-known characters around here. We're very old friends.'

'Mebbe more than that,' Don Saunders mused, his dark eyes passing up and down Bart's immaculate attire. 'You're Bart Meredith, I s'pose – from Boston. Jane's been tellin' me about you. Shake.'

Bart's right hand was gripped in such iron-strong fingers that he nearly took a back somersault into the apple barrel. Finally he disentangled his hand and gave a grudging nod of greeting.

'An excellent turn-out, son,' Meredith remarked. 'I'll now see what I can do for myself.'

'Go ahead,' Bart growled, and looked grimly again at Don Saunders.

'No offence, stranger,' Saunders said drily. 'But in that outfit you look about as comfortable as a bronc wearin' a saddle for the first time.'

'Maybe that's just how I do feel!' Bart retorted.

Saunders straightened up and glanced at the girl.

'Be seein' you around, Jane,' he said. 'Same goes for you, tenderfoot.' Then with long strides he left the store, his single gun smacking against his heavy thigh. Bart stared after him.

'Can't say I like that guy,' he growled.

'Don? Oh, he's all right – he's rich, and an important man in this town, as well as being perhaps its fastest shooter. He's inclined to bully those who can't stand up to him. Natural arrogance, I suppose.'

'What did he mean by you and he being more than friends?'

'Just talk,' Jane said lightly; then she added: 'Take care you never cross Don, Bart. He'll kill you if you do. There's never been a man in this region who could stand up to him. On the right side of him he's OK; otherwise watch out.'

Bart tightened his lips, looked again towards the store doorway, then at the man behind the counter. He gave the girl a nudge.

'Where do I get a gun – or guns – around here? This guy sell them?'

'Uh-huh. I'd recommend thirty-eights. Forty-fives would be too heavy for you, I'm afraid.'

Bart strode to the counter, his jaw set. 'Show me a couple of forty-fives and make them good ones.'

For several minutes he examined the various guns which were shown him, not understanding a thing about them, finally selecting a pair of twin .45s which the girl insisted were just right for him. He put them in their shiny holsters and strapped the cartridge belts crosswise so a gun hung at either thigh. An unusual heaviness hung in the region of his stomach as he moved about stiffly.

'Now you look right,' Jane decided, approvingly. 'The only thing you have to do now is stand up straight and move about easily.'

'Which isn't so. . .' Bart stopped, gazing blankly towards the adjoining room as his father came through the door-way. The girl looked too and for all her self-control she could not help laughing outright.

'Is there something incongruous, Miss Jane?' Meredith inquired, coming to a halt beside the counter.

'After seeing you,' Bart chuckled, 'I don't feel nearly as conspicuous.'

Meredith was wearing riding-breeches and a vivid blue flannel shirt, a broad belt emphasizing the enormity of his middle. Half-boots with white clocks up the sides fitted snugly on his unusually small feet. The red kerchief was tossed carelessly sideways. But what upset the entire ensemble was his own Homburg hat, perched dead centre on his semi-bald head.

'That will have to come off,' Bart decided, staring at it.

'No, son!' Meredith was stonily adamant. 'This hat is a mark of respect to your mother. I wore a black Homburg to her funeral – and I shall continue to wear one. Only in the remainder shall I conform to Western attire.' He turned. 'My man, some weapons, please. Preferably thirty-eights. I prefer the smaller-calibre gun for comfortable trigger action.'

Bart gazed at him and then at the girl. 'To hear him talk you'd think he'd been born out here!' he exclaimed.

Imperturbably, Meredith selected twin .38s, put them in

the holsters, then strapped the cartridge belts across his vast paunch.

Bart paid the bill and then followed the girl to the boardwalk outside, his father coming up in the rear. He looked out onto the busy street.

'What happens now? Should I go and see the sheriff and see what he intends doing concerning my brother's remains – if any – and the fire-raising last night? Oughtn't there to be an inquest or something?'

'Normally, yes,' Jane agreed, 'but recently there have been so many killings in this valley that it would have been impossible to keep track of the inquests and bodies. I'm afraid that the business will just be written off as another unsolved tragedy. If anything is discovered it will be by you and your father, because Dave was family and you have a definite interest in seeing justice done.'

Meredith cleared his throat and stepped forward.

'If I might make a suggestion, son? I think that we should join forces with the terrorists on their next raid. Become part of them and, in the local idiom, try and discover "what's cooking".'

'How the devil do you suppose we could join forces with them, Dad? We'd be shot to bits before we could get within a few yards!'

'Hear me out, son. I believe we might be able to capture two men in the gang whose dimensions approximate our own. Inevitably these men will be masked – probably with kerchiefs – so if we are masked too and take their places, and their clothes if need be, no one will know by night but what we *are* them.'

As Bart hesitated, Meredith turned to the girl.

'I am assuming, Miss Jane, that these terrorists usually approach from some fixed direction? Say, perhaps, the mountains?'

'They do seem to come from there,' Jane agreed. 'I think their hideout is up there somewhere, but since they can snipe anybody off who approaches it's too dangerous to go and look – as far as the sheriff and his boys are concerned, that is.'

'All right,' Meredith said. 'We ride out towards the mountains, select a convenient spot where we can hide – at a point where the terrorists are bound to cross to reach this valley, and then select two men who resemble us in build. After, we shall take their places. In that way we may at least learn who the ringleader is and can lay our plans accordingly.'

'The whole thing's crazy!' Bart protested. 'I can't ride a horse or shoot a gun properly, and a lariat to me is just a piece of rope with which I'd probably strangle myself – and you suggest we overpower two tough outlaws and take their places!'

There was stony silence for a moment. It hurt Bart much more than any volley of words. He felt himself squirming at the steady look Jane gave him.

'The plan's perfect, Mr Meredith,' she commented. 'It's one sure way of trying to find the ringleader of this gang.'

'But I'm still raw to the game!' Bart protested.

'I didn't say act *immediately*, son,' Meredith pointed out. 'It will probably be a few days before there is another raid. In the interval you can undergo training in horse riding, shooting, and throwing a lariat. I will gladly pass on what smattering of knowledge I have and I am sure Miss Jane will not withhold her own bag of tricks.'

'I'll teach you everything I know,' Jane affirmed. 'At least make you capable of looking after yourself. I want you to prove yourself a man, Bart,' she added seriously. 'I'm sure you can.'

'One thing, son,' Meredith broke in quietly. 'This scheme should be kept exclusively just between the three of us. A mere chance word or hint might undo everything and endanger our very lives.'

'True enough,' the girl admitted, frowning. 'Yes, we'll keep it to ourselves – even from my stepfather. He's often drinking and sometimes gambling in the Painted Lady and he might let something slip quite unintentionally. I'll simply tell him that – er – you and Bart have decided to go into action or something.'

'How about getting back to the ranch now?' Bart glanced down at the horses beside the tie rail. 'Seems to me it's time we had something to eat.'

'And drink?' Jane asked drily, but Bart shook his head.

'I've gone without so far: I might as well stay that way.'

4

KIDNAPPED

For a week, as circumstances forced him to live the life of a Westerner, Bart Meredith spent most of his waking hours with Jane and his father, usually in the sun-baked pasture-land owned by Mike Farnon. Here, without any embarrassment, he was able to discover the tricks necessary to ride a horse properly, and once he had mastered the art he was agreeably surprised to discover how much he enjoyed himself. So intent was he that he failed to notice how he was gradually changing, both mentally and physically, under the combined influence of the girl and local geography. Sunlight and fresh air, ample food and hard exercise, were adding pounds to his stature and stamina. Now and again he felt a nagging urge to dash to the Painted Lady for a stiff drink – then he overcame it and stayed right where he was.

At the end of the week his horsemanship was passable, his gunplay fair, and his rope-throwing mediocre. Mastering a lariat, the girl pointed out, was the work of years. She herself was an expert, as she demonstrated by roping a steer. His father, however, counterbalanced this deficiency by proving himself remarkably adept with the coil.

'I think,' Jane said, on the evening of the seventh day, 'that from now on it's just a matter of practice. With your father beside you I feel doubly confident you can look after yourself.'

'Thank you, Miss Jane,' Meredith murmured, peering under his hat brim into the incredible sunset. 'So tonight we start looking for a convenient spot to hide out to waylay – when the next raid is made – a couple of outlaws, and take their place.'

Overhead the evening sky changed almost imperceptibly, salmon-pink and mauve feathers spreading across the blue – like frost on an icy windowpane.

'We'd better be getting inside,' the girl decided. She turned and led the way into the ranch. Her stepfather greeted them as they came trooping in.

'Still tryin' to ride that bronco, Bart?' Farnon asked with a smile.

'Not trying – riding it,' Jane responded, with not a little pride. 'I've managed to teach him how.'

No more was said and all three parted to wash and freshen up. Later, over the evening meal Mike Farnon asked a question.

'When are you goin' off on this secret mission you keep talkin' about, Bart?'

'My father and I will be leaving tonight.'

Mike Farnon sat back and considered, brooding thought on his strongly cut face.

'And what exactly are you figurin' to do?'

'I'm afraid our plan must remain secret,' Meredith said. 'It relies on certain essential details which a chance word might completely upset. I hope you understand.'

'Well,' Farnon smiled faintly, 'if you want to be mysterious there ain't nothin' I can do to stop it. My gal here know anythin' about your plan?'

'I only know they're going on a mission,' Jane said, shrugging.

'She's not coming with us,' Bart added. 'This is a job for men alone.'

Farnon did not say anything but for just a moment Bart thought he saw a suggestion of contempt in the bright blue eyes. He frowned to himself and continued with his meal.

It was close on ten o'clock when Bart and his father both rose from the table.

'We're leaving,' Bart said. 'We may not be back tonight. Depends on what happens and what we do.'

'OK either way,' Farnon said. 'Good luck.'

Jane rose too and accompanied the two men as far as the yard. In the twilight she stood looking at them both as they unfastened their horses from the tie rail. Faintly against the western afterglow she could see Meredith's amazing Homburg and Bart's big Stetson.

'You're starting out to be a man tonight, Bart,' she murmured, grasping his hand.

At that moment her upturned face was eminently kissable – but Bart resisted temptation and contented himself with pressing her hand in return. Then he climbed up into the saddle.

The two men went out through the yard gateway and across the sweep of twilit pastureland which led to the main trail. When they were well out of sight of the ranch house Brad drew rein.

'It's no use, Dad, I can't tackle this business without a bracer!'

'Am I to understand that you wish to have a drink?' There was hurt in Meredith's voice.

'Not wish – I'm *going* to! I've got to get some whiskey inside me before I fall apart. I've kept off it ever since we

51

got into this confounded country, but I just can't stand it any more. It's only ten-fifteen so the Painted Lady will still be open.'

'Miss Jane won't like hearing that you went for a drink, son.'

'It's something stronger than myself, or my regard for Jane. I've just got to have a drink. Come on!'

Since argument was useless Meredith swung his horse's head round and followed Bart as far as the trail. Then without either of them exchanging words they completed the journey to Mountain Peak and dismounted outside Don Saunders' saloon. Meredith regarded the lighted windows and listened with obvious distaste to the clamour floating from beyond the batwings.

'The fleshpots of the West,' he observed, somewhat ambiguously, tying the horses' reins to the hitch rail.

'Fact remains I need a drink,' Bart said stubbornly. He pushed open the batwings and stood looking the saloon over. Meredith came in silently behind him and stood gazing too.

At this hour the Painted Lady was about at the height of the evening's business, and thickly clouded with tobacco fumes. At the tables were cattle-dealers, punchers, half-breeds, Mexicans, and sundry women: some ordinary, others overdressed and painted; others painted and decidedly under-dressed. The noise was appalling. To the rattle of poker chips and the excitement at the faro and roulette tables was added the sound of argumentative voices, some inflamed by liquor, the tinny discord of a three-piece orchestra on a rostrum at the far end of the saloon, and the struggle of a heavy-breasted middle-aged woman in a sequin gown to sing a soprano song. After the fresh air of the night, sweet with the tang of juniper and cedars, the atmosphere in here positively stank.

Meredith drew himself up with portly dignity as he realized that several men and women were looking at him and grinning. They began talking amongst themselves or behind their hands, and the infection seemed to spread to every man and woman in the saloon as Bart walked across to the bar counter with his father behind him.

'What'll it be?' the barkeep asked, putting down a cloth.

'Double whiskey,' Bart responded.

'And one ginger beer,' Meredith added.

The barkeep's mouth opened slightly and he surveyed the moonlike face and Homburg hat. Muttering beneath his breath, he turned to the back bar. In a moment or two the double whiskey and ginger beer were planked down and Bart handed over the payment.

'I'm drinking this stuff just to keep you company,' Meredith pointed out. 'Not because I have a liking for creating gas in the stomach!'

'Any gas in yours would be lost,' Bart grinned, then he swallowed off the whisky and breathed a deep sigh of satisfaction. 'Ah! That's more like it!'

He ordered another double and was about to raise it to his lips when he paused, looking across the saloon. In the distance, leaning against one of the ornate pillars, stood Don Saunders, smoking a black cheroot. His dark hair, now he was without hat, gleamed softly in the oil-lights. He gave no indication as to whether he had seen Bart and his father.

'Say, stranger, who's this character?' a gruff voiced asked.

Bart gave a start and found himself looking at a swarthy puncher with a scarred right cheek, one of three men seated at a nearby table with drinks and cards in front of them. Apparently they had been engaged in a poker game.

'Talking to me?' Bart asked.

'Yeah. Who's the critter in the fancy hat? Ain't never seen anythin' like it afore in these parts.'

'The name, my good man, is Meredith,' Bart's father responded coldly, putting down his glass.

'Huh?' The puncher looked blank. 'He talks, too! A perishin' Easterner, judgin' by the accent . . .'

The puncher got to his feet – a tall, lean-boned individual about Bart's own build. With fingers resting on the butt of his right-hand Colt he came across to the bar counter and sized Meredith up carefully. Then his gaze moved to Bart as he stood watching somewhat uncertainly.

'This go with you?' the puncher inquired. 'Sort of looks after you?'

'He's my father,' Bart retorted. 'What's it got to do with you?'

'Plenty. We don't like your sort around here – a dude and his minder ain't cut out for Mountain Peak. In this town we live only if we're fit to – not by carryin' a wet nurse around.'

'It would seem,' Meredith observed, 'that you wish to pick an unprovoked quarrel. I think you are one of the men who murdered my son David and burned down his ranch?'

'What the hell you talkin' about, fatty?' the puncher snapped. 'You callin' me a killer?'

'We couldn't identify the gangsters we encountered because they wore face-masks – but you could know *us* again quite easily. Seeking to square accounts with us in this way identifies you as one of the terrorist gang!'

The puncher stared. 'You're loco! I ain't no gang member, I'm a puncher in the Top C outfit and I ain't standin' for no lip from a pot-bellied Easterner like you neither!'

Suddenly the man whipped out his gun, but simultaneously Meredith's enormous stomach butted forward with tremendous violence. It took the puncher clean in the midriff, and such was the force behind it he seemed to rebound; he fell backwards into the table and knocked it flying. He came to rest on his back, poker chips and cards around him and spilled beer trickling down his face.

The puncher grabbed at his fallen gun and whirled it up, then he had to stop as the hand of Don Saunders suddenly descended and clamped about his wrist.

'Take it easy, Josh,' Saunders said briefly. 'Get on your feet and cool down.'

'But this low-down critter knocked me for—'

'On your feet!' Saunders snapped, and dragged the puncher upwards. 'Any more trouble and you'll answer to me.'

Sullenly the puncher reholstered his gun and then helped his colleagues to straighten the table. Saunders turned and strolled over to the bar where Bart and his father stood watching.

'Not doin' so good, stranger, are you?' Saunders observed. 'Can't even stand up for yourself.'

Bart finished his whiskey and put the glass down.

'No reason to. That guy's remarks weren't addressed to me.'

'Supposin' they had been? Would you have done anythin'?'

'Any concern of yours what I do?' Bart demanded.

'It is when you're in my place. I'm not used to customers who can't act like men. Namby-pambies have no place around here. I think you'd both be safer at that table in the corner there. I'll have some drinks sent over to you – with my compliments.'

'Not for me,' Meredith protested, raising a hand.

'Make mine a double whiskey then,' Bart said. 'Thanks for the treat.'

Don Saunders grinned cynically. 'With some whiskey in your belly you may act a bit more as though you've got guts.'

His father following behind him, Bart pushed his way through the midst of the tables and the seated men and women, eventually settling down in a far corner seat near the noisy little three-piece orchestra. Meredith sat down too, puffed gently to himself, and then placed his hat carefully under his chair.

'That, son, will make three double whiskeys.'

'What of it?' Bart snapped. 'Maybe it *will* put some manhood into me, as friend Saunders said. God knows, I could do with it. And I'll drink as much as I want, and be damned to you!'

'Are you forgetting we came out tonight to go on a mission? A clear head is absolutely necessary, and—'

'You suggesting I'm tight?'

'You're becoming argumentative – a sure sign.'

Bart pushed his hat up on his forehead and rubbed his hands in satisfaction as the waiter brought over his drink. He toyed with the glass for a moment and then raised it to his lips, watched by his father's coldly disapproving eyes. Then Bart paused, staring towards the bar.

'I'll be damned! Jane, of all people! Here!'

Meredith turned and gazed through the fumes. There was no mistaking Jane Talbot in her check shirt, riding trousers, and half-boots, her wealth of blonde hair flowing free – just as there was no mistaking that Don Saunders had his arm about her slim shoulders and was guiding her to a quiet corner of the saloon.

Fixedly Bart watched them, his drink forgotten in his hand. Meredith watched also, and saw that the big saloon-owner was becoming violently possessive about something. With his arm now encircling the girl's waist he seemed to be doing his best to kiss her, despite her protests. The men and women at the tables, evidently used to this kind of thing – or else knowing better than to interfere with the fastest triggerman in town – took not the least notice.

'Miss Jane's in trouble, son!'

'Serves her right, doesn't it?' Bart's voice was bitter. 'The moment my back's turned she's here, wrapped up in Saunders' arms. No wonder he said he and Jane were more than friends.'

'That's how it *looks*, but actually she may have no wish to—'

'Oh, shut up! She made a play for me and the moment she thinks I'm out of the way she spends her time with the guy who really means something to her.' Bart grinned cynically as he watched the distant vision of the girl struggling in Saunders' arms. 'Make a man of me, eh? I'll damned well show *her*!'

He picked up his whiskey and gulped it down quickly. Then he motioned to a hovering waiter. 'Another – and make it quick.'

The man nodded and went over to the bar. Meredith sat watching Jane and the saloon-owner for a moment, then he got to his feet.

'Miss Jane needs help!'

'Do what you like. Why should I care?'

Meredith picked up his hat from under the chair, set it squarely on his head, and pushed amidst the tables until he came to the corner where Jane was striving to break free of Saunders' embrace.

'Don, for heaven's sake, you're hurting—!' she gasped out. 'Let me go!'

'If we've got to part I'm surely entitled to a goodbye

kiss?' Saunders grinned. ' 'Specially as you're desertin' me for a tenderfoot.'

'Better unhand the lady,' Meredith said, halting a couple of feet away.

Saunders turned, blinked, and released the girl slowly, more in surprise than anything else. The girl looked at Meredith in a mixture of amazement and relief. Then she caught hold of his arm.

'What are you doing here, Mr Meredith? I thought you and Bart had gone off somewhere.'

'My son is over there, at a far corner. I regret to say that he found it necessary to have several "bracers" before starting off. Then we saw you . . .'

'Thank heaven you did.' Jane looked at Saunders bitterly. 'I'm just about bruised all over . . .'

'Listen, you!' Saunders whirled on Meredith with his gun levelled. Anger had now replaced surprise. 'I'm going to make you dance as you've never danced before. Start right now!'

The revolver exploded deafeningly and a bullet buried itself in the floor not an inch from Meredith's left foot. Instantly everybody in the room turned to look.

'Don, please . . .' Jane clutched Saunders' hand only to be whirled violently against the wall.

'*Dance!*' Saunders yelled, and fired twice more.

Meredith shifted his feet, but he did not dance. Instead his right foot rose and then came down with savage violence on Saunders' toes. He gave a yelp of anguish as eighteen stone literally jumped on him, and at the same moment Meredith butted forward his huge equator and lashed up his right fist. Saunders, big though he was, stood no chance. He overbalanced, clung desperately to the dried palm in the corner, missed his hold, and finished up with the broken pottery, soil, and plant scattered on top of him. With a clatter the revolver bounced from his hand on to the floor.

'Why, you dirty . . .'

As Saunders began to scramble to his feet Meredith abruptly snatched out his right-hand gun and levelled it implacably.

Saunders breathed hard and scooped back his dishevelled hair. Savagely he thrust his gun back into its holster.

'OK, you win,' he snapped. 'Mebbe I'm wasting my time with that one anyways.'

'You are,' Meredith agreed; then, taking Jane's arm, he led her through the midst of the staring men and women. They were obviously finding it difficult to assimilate the fact that an overweight Easterner had bested the fastest triggerman in Mountain Peak.

'I'm grateful,' Jane said anxiously, looking at him, 'but I wish you hadn't done that. You've made an enemy out of Don Saunders. One day, when you least expect it, he may draw a gun on you.'

Meredith shrugged. 'I can take care of myself.'

In a moment or two she and Meredith reached the table where Bart was sitting. He looked up at her blearily, then at his father.

'Fancy yourself as an outsize Sir Galahad, Dad?' he asked cynically.

'Hardly a matter of that, son. Miss Jane was—'

'Oh, shut up!' Bart interrupted impatiently, and swallowed down the remainder of his drink. 'An' leave me alone – both of you!'

'Bart, what's the *matter* with you?' Jane seized his shoulder and shook it violently. 'Look at me! What are you doing here when you should be out with your father on your mission?'

'I came here for a drink,' Bart said, speaking with the

deliberation of a man with intoxicant in his tongue. 'An' it's jus' as well I did, it seems. Next thing I see is you in Don Saunders' arms. Sort of makes it pointless for me to try an' look like a man in your eyes, doesn't it?'

'But Bart, all I came here for was—'

'I don't want to hear it!' Bart interrupted hotly. 'I saw you – an' I can believe what I see. Just leave me alone!'

'All right, we'll go,' Jane agreed bitterly. 'Obviously no use talking to a man when he's . . . roostered!'

She swung away in fury, but Bart did not look up to watch her. Meredith sighed and followed behind the girl. When they had reached the boardwalk she looked at him sharply.

'Why didn't you stop him drinking?' she demanded. 'He's pretty nearly under the table.'

'Originally he came for just one drink,' Meredith sighed, considering the kerosene-lighted street. 'But there was some kind of a fracas with a cowpuncher and it resulted in Mr Saunders making him a present of a second drink. Then, when he saw you in his arms he went to pieces. Not uncommon for a man with a deep regard for a woman to drown himself in drink when he finds she doesn't really mean what she says.'

'Who doesn't?' Jane demanded. 'What on earth are you talking about?'

Meredith gave a sad smile. 'Surely, it's obvious? We both saw you and Mr Saunders—'

'And both jumped to conclusions! How typically, idiotically man-like! All I came here for was to tell Don Saunders that I've decided to break things off with him. Not that they were ever very serious, anyway – but I felt it only right to tell him that sort of thing was finished, both in fairness to him and because I . . . find Bart means a good deal to me.'

Meredith fondled his chins. 'That would certainly explain why you went to all that trouble to try and make something of him . . . So Mr Saunders' attentions, and his remarks as I approached him, were intended as a farewell?'

'Yes – but it turned nasty. You arrived just in time. Don isn't really bad, just possessive. Being rich and powerful, he thinks he can take liberties, particularly with women. Nothing more to it than that . . . if only Bart had been sober enough to listen to me.'

'He will be in time,' Meredith said calmly. 'He's very fond of you, though he tries to appear quite unconcerned. Just natural pride because you yourself have not given him any open encouragement for him to express his affection for you.'

'I don't want him to know,' Jane explained seriously. 'First I want him to find out that he is a real man: the rest can follow. If once he finds his feet I'm willing to wager he'll become one of the toughest men in the town, the kind of man a girl of this region could really love with all her heart.'

'Nicely put,' Meredith commented, then after a glance back towards the busy saloon he added: 'Apparently he's not coming after us so I think we had better return home. Our excursion will have to be abandoned, at least for the time being.'

'He'll come round to it when he knows the facts,' Jane said, the last traces of her anger disappearing. 'I'm sure of it.'

Meredith held her pinto for her as she mounted, then swung into the saddle of his own sorrel. Side by side they began the journey down the high street, which led presently to the trail and out under the stars, the breath of the night wind blowing across the pastureland.

Abruptly Meredith drew his horse to a sudden stop. He sat motionless, a hand raised slightly in the starlight and his whole bearing intent. Jane also stopped her pinto and waited.

'Just for a moment I heard something – horses' hoofs,' Meredith told the girl. 'Could have been from the pasture on our right here.'

Jane glanced about her uneasily in the gloom. 'If it's those terrorists – Look out!' she finished in alarm, and spurred her horse simultaneously.

Her intention of making a dash for it, however, was not realized. Suddenly the trail was alive with men. Evidently they had been hidden behind the thick bushes skirting the trail and the sound of one of them, perhaps arriving later than the others, had been what Meredith had heard. Now he and the girl found themselves surrounded, dragged from their horses, and flung unceremoniously into the dust. None of the men spoke, nor were their faces in the least visible with kerchiefs drawn up to the eyes.

Desperately though he struggled and fought, Meredith was utterly outnumbered. His guns were taken from him, he was struck savagely several times, then finally bound with a tough lariat and flung violently into the ditch at the side of the trail. He landed face up amidst weeds and grass and was just able to see the hapless Jane struggling in the midst of the men as she was borne away to the pastureland. A few moments later there followed the hollow reverberation of horses' hoofs hurtling across the earth – and at last silence. The night was still.

The dirty coyotes! Meredith thought furiously. The moment I heard them I should have fired and asked questions afterwards—

He began a fierce struggle to tear free of the cord holding him. At the end of ten minutes, resting at intervals, he had almost freed one hand – then at the sound of an approaching horse he looked up. He dared not cry out until he was sure it was not another terrorist.

Presently the lone horseman came into view in the dawning moonrise, half-slumped over in his saddle, as though he slept whilst he rode.

'*Bart!*' Meredith shouted hoarsely. 'Give me a hand, son – *Hey, there!*'

Bart took not the least notice of him. His horse carried him on down the trail and was lost to sight.

'Tight to the wide,' Meredith muttered. 'Blast the man who invented liquor . . .' and then with a mighty wrench he tore his right hand free.

5

NIGHT SKIRMISH

In something like a half-stupor Bart managed to put his mare in the stable and then stumbled up the steps into the Slanting F ranch house.

As he entered the living-room he blinked in the oil-light and found Mike Farnon staring at him.

'Where have you been, Bart?' he demanded, and there seemed to be both relief and anger in his tone.

'None of your business,' Bart growled. 'Jus' thought I'd let you know I've come back ... That father of mine got here yet?'

'Not yet, but ...'

'Then I'm goin' to bed. 'Night.'

'Wait a darned minute!' Farnon gripped him by the shoulders and whirled him around. 'Something's happened to Jane! She's been snatched by the terrorists! Take a look at this. It was just thrown through the open window here. It nearly hit me ...'

Bart took the note and squinted at it. It was heavily creased from where it had been round a stone. He pinched finger and thumb in his eyes and then shook his head.

'No use to me . . . I can't read it. My eyes are dancing—'

'You mean you're that brimful of liquor you can't stand up!' Farnon interrupted angrily. 'The note says that my gal's been taken away by the outlaws – and she'll stay away unless I'm willin' to hand over five thousand dollars. I've got to pin the answer on the big sycamore tree west of the trail from here.' Again his hands shook Bart violently. 'Blast you, man, wake up! Are you even listenin'?'

'Uh-huh,' Bart assented sleepily. 'But I jus' don't care. I saw tonight the kind of girl she is – an' I don't want to have anything more to do with her. She's your responsibility – I'm going to bed.'

'But you can't! I'm going to try and find her and I need help badly. I'm not young enough to tackle these jobs on my own. Get the liquor squeezed out of yourself, feller, and come with me.'

Bart shook his head, slouched across the room unsteadily, and opened the door of his bedroom. He paused and looked back.

'I'm gettin' out in the mornin',' he slurred. 'I know when I've outstayed my welcome.' Then he went into the room and shut the door. He had only the vaguest idea where the bed was but somehow he found it and fell upon it heavily. Almost immediately he was asleep.

He awakened again at a violent shaking of his shoulder. Uneasily he stirred and passed a tongue over parched lips.

'What the hell's wrong?' he demanded irritably, then shut his eyes as quickly as he had opened them. 'And turn out that confounded oil-lamp! It hurts!'

'It's me – your father! You've got to listen to me!'

'Since when? Go to sleep and stop pestering me!'

'Wake up, damn you! This is important!'

The shaking became so violent that Bart had no alternative other than to sit up. Holding his aching head, he opened his eyes and then gave a start. His father's round, chubby face was battered and bruised.

'For the love of Mike, what happened to *you*?'

'Are you – sober?' Meredith asked urgently, gripping his son's arms. Bart grinned faintly.

'As a judge. I must have slept off the effect. What's gone wrong?'

'You've been asleep for about an hour, according to Farnon. He's pacing the next room like a caged tiger, waiting for you, or me, or both of us to go with him and try and find Miss Jane. She's been kidnapped!'

'Yes, I remember that bit,' Bart muttered. 'So what? She doesn't mean anything to me any more.'

'But she does!' Meredith insisted. 'I talked to her before we were attacked by terrorists and she was captured – and you have the whole thing wrong.' He went into every detail, finishing: 'She loves you, you damned fool! She just wants you to act like a man, if only to protect yourself.'

Bart was silent for a moment, considering, rubbing his face slowly and working the blur out of his eyes.

'OK, that does it!' he said. 'I've never known you to lie to me, Dad. I've been about the biggest idiot going, it seems – it's got to end, and quickly! If any damned terrorists think they can hold Jane they're vastly mistaken.'

Meredith's bruised face would have beamed, only the damage to it prevented any expression.

'That's what I've been wanting to hear, son! I'll go and tell Mr Farnon.'

Bart wasted no time in getting into his boots, then he swamped his face and neck in cold water to help revive himself. Grim-faced he went into the living-room. Mike Farnon turned to look at him.

'Glad you've come round – mighty glad,' he said earnestly. 'Now I can get after my stepdaughter with you two helpin' me.'

'Fortunately,' Meredith said, settling his hat firmly, 'those terrorists didn't take my guns with them. They only threw them away. Once I'd freed myself I found them lying in the grass, together with Miss Jane's thirty-two.' He put it on the table and Bart looked at it sickly.

'For her sake, the sooner we locate her the better,' Meredith resumed, as Bart took his Stetson from the door and put it on. 'One thing puzzles me,' he added, 'how did the terrorists know that she would be riding back from town with me? Who tipped them off?'

'Simple enough,' Mike Farnon said, his voice grim. 'They probably saw you and your son leave here – and Jane shortly after you – to go into town. Then they decided to lie in wait for you coming back; or else the man who's back of this terror gang is Don Saunders and he tipped off his boys to get busy, seein' as Jane had just told him she was through with him.'

'Something else a bit queer, too,' Bart said. 'I wonder why they were satisfied with just beating you up, Dad? Particularly after the way you manhandled Saunders – if he's back of it.'

'They probably thought they had left me for dead, son. Certainly they knocked me about enough, but I'm blubbery and not so easy to kill as one would imagine. They wouldn't shoot me because bullets can be identified when taken from a body.'

'Let's go!' Bart said urgently. 'Jane's life is in danger with every second we delay. Any idea which direction we should take, Mr Farnon?'

'Nothin' definite, but it seems likely that those jiggers can't hide any place but in the mountains – so we'd better head there. I've got the horses waitin' outside.'

In a few minutes all three were speeding swiftly across

the pastures, their way illumined by the risen moon. As they went Bart felt his head clearing remarkably from the fogs of the liquor he had consumed – and there was something different stirring in his soul, too.

For a moment he felt again that indefinable sense of exhilaration begotten of these great spaces. The knowledge that Jane really cared for him beneath the exterior of aloofness she had shown pointed to the fact that, for the first time in his life, he must become a man.

After twenty minutes of hard riding, the base of the foothills was reached. Mike Farnon slowed the pace and twisted round in his saddle.

'Better take it easy around here, fellers,' he cautioned. 'This moon's helped us up to now to see our way, but from here on it'll be an enemy. Like as not the outlaws will have a look-out stationed somewhere, and he'll not have much trouble spottin' us. Keep to the shadows as much as possible.'

The two men nodded and followed behind the rancher as he allowed his horse to pick its way through the treacherous rubble and stones forming the mountain foothills. Since Farnon had spent all his life in the district Bart felt that he was safe in trusting to him to find the outlaws' lair. Certainly he knew he could not do any better himself.

The way went ever upwards, chiefly following an arroyo, which, Farnon explained, was the most likely trail that anybody hiding in the mountains would follow. Though the pursuit of the old watercourse left them with no cover, and so easily visible targets in the moonlight to any watching eyes – nothing happened. Presently they came into a region of cedar and juniper trees. The sound of the wind sighing through their heavy branches was only drowned now and again by the eager gurgling of a freshet plunging amidst the rocks as the three horsemen negotiated their way.

Higher and higher still, beyond the region of the trees to the areas where moonlight made strange patterns and fancies of the sleeping wilderness of loco-weeds and buckbean. Until in time even these were left behind and only the mountains remained – climbing on top of each other in merciless crags and buttresses into the utter violet of the night sky. So clear was the air, so sharp the highest spires of the mountains, they seemed to be scraping the stars as they hung out of the void like the lanterns of God.

They continued the ascent until they reached a narrow pathway skirting the edge of the mountain, with a 300 feet drop into a gorge on one side of it. Abruptly Farnon drew to a halt and pointed.

'Take it easy,' he breathed. 'Look!'

Distinctly outlined against the stars and moonlit sky, perhaps a quarter of a mile ahead of them, was a lone figure perched on a high rock. They could faintly descry that he was turning slowly, surveying the view, the outline of his big-brimmed hat the most clearly marked thing about him.

'Down,' Farnon murmured. 'Off our horses before he spots us.'

Promptly the men slid from their saddles then drew their horses gently after them as they sought the rock concealment at the side of the trail. Evidently they had not been spotted for there was no sound of a sudden whanging bullet.

'We've struck their hide-out, anyways,' Farnon said. 'Now we have to figure how to rescue Jane and then beat it without bullets in our hides. We might manage it if we can take care of the look-out perched up there. Think you could fix him, Bart?'

'You mean shoot him?' Bart asked.

'Hell, no! The noise of the shot would be the finish for

us. No, I mean silence him – somehow. Take somebody agile and strong to do it – like you. Beyond me at my age.'

As Bart hesitated, his father spoke up. 'I think you can leave this to me, son.'

'Go to it then,' Bart said promptly. 'But be careful!'

They secured their horses to spurs of rock and then began a stealthy advance, dodging from rock to rock and coming ever nearer the exceptionally high one where the sentry stood. At last they were within fifty feet of him, still without his having noticed them. Then Meredith put his plan into action.

With surprising silence considering his bulk he glided forward amidst the rocks, paused, and then began a silent detour round the huge pinnacle on which the sentry stood, using its overhanging bulk for cover. Presently he came to the other side of it and here found it less sheer with plenty of footholds. Motionless, frozen amidst the rocks, Meredith stood watching keenly until the sentry was looking in the opposite direction – then in sudden swift movements he vaulted up the rock and made a mighty grab at the man's ankles before he could realize what had happened.

Before he could yell a warning Meredith sat on him with his full weight. Thus pinned and with the crushing load on his stomach the puncher could hardly move, let alone shout – and his silence was finally assured as Meredith ripped off the man's kerchief and bound it tightly into his mouth. Then taking his guns from the holsters he threw them as far as he could into the moonlit canyon twenty feet away.

The man struggled fiercely, then he broke off with a choking gasp as Meredith's fist suddenly struck him with shattering force on the right side of the jaw. It was a smooth, deliberate, perfectly-timed blow delivered with all

Meredith's elephantine strength. The man relaxed, completely knocked out.

Meredith heaved the man to his feet, stood him up, then delivered a well-aimed kick at his rear. He keeled off the rock and dropped like a sack of cement amidst the rubble and dirt a few feet below.

'Nice work,' Bart said, coming up the rock with Mike Farnon close behind him. 'We saw every bit of it. But what's next?'

'I think we should try and take 'em by surprise,' Farnon answered, peering about him in the moonlight. 'Their hide-out must be nearby. Yes, take a look!' he broke off, pointing. 'There's a fire there, in one of those mountain caves.'

Bart and his father saw it distinctly for a moment – a flickering a couple of hundred yards distant, then it vanished again as somebody evidently came in front of it.

'I would suggest a decoy,' Meredith said, thinking. 'The best course would be to creep up near the cave, fire a lot of shots and make a lot of noise – giving the impression of quite a number of gunmen approaching – then whilst they're distracted I will dash into the cave and try to find Miss Jane.'

'*You* will?' Bart asked.

'Look, son, I'm a better gunman than you if it comes to it. You and Mr Farnon will be the decoys whilst I do what I can.'

Moving silently amidst the rocks, they worked their way round until they were within a hundred yards of the cave mouth. From this vantage point they could see straight into it. There was a flickering fire, somewhat imperfectly shielded, and beyond it a blur of faces.

'Count up to twenty and then start firing – and after-wards go back to the horses,' Meredith instructed. 'If all else fails I'll rejoin you at the ranch.'

He crept forward amidst the rocks until he had reached the edge of the cave-mouth. Motionless, he took stock of the position.

There were about eight men sprawled in different parts of the cave, some of them smoking, others just gazing towards the fire. To Meredith's annoyance the firelight was not bright enough to reveal features. Then his eyes narrowed. In the remoter depths of the cave, seated on the floor with her back to the wall, was Jane. She seemed to be bound.

So much he had time to observe, then there came the explosion of revolver shots for which he was waiting, the noise echoing violently in the mountains. Immediately the triggermen inside the cave scrambled to their feet, whipping their guns from their holsters and tumbling over one another to get to the pathway. Meredith kept flat against the wall, trusting to the shadows.

'A big party comin' from the sound of it,' one of the men snapped. 'We'd best go see—'

'Len's gone!' another one exclaimed, astonished. 'Last I saw of him he was on that rock, posted to give us the tip off . . .'

There were more reports of gunfire and the men pressed on urgently, drawing up their kerchiefs to their faces as they moved. In all, Meredith noted that six of them dashed off to investigate, which left him with two to deal with. He did not even hesitate. He drew his guns and moved swiftly into the cave, surprising the two remaining triggermen before they had a chance to level their weapons at him.

'Outside!' Meredith commanded. Far from obeying the men ignored the guns he held and dived at him.

Not wishing to draw attention by firing he side-stepped

at the last moment and brought the revolvers down butt-foremost on each man's neck in turn. The left-hand man he stunned completely: the other dodged and swung round, then he gave a howl of anguish as with a sweeping kick of his foot Meredith footballed blazing red ashes into the man's face. Before he had a chance to recover Meredith had swung the gun-butt again, cracking the man on top of the skull. He dropped with a thud and lay motionless.

Breathing hard, Meredith dashed across to where the girl lay watching anxiously. In ten seconds he had the ropes away and hauled her to her feet.

'Mr Meredith! How—?'

'No time to talk! Outside – quickly!'

Meredith grabbed her arm and propelled her out of the cave and along the uneven trail along the mountain side. He glanced back as he went but there seemed to be little going on, and the uneasy calm lasted until the horses were reached. Bart and Farnon had worked their way back and were waiting anxiously.

'You got her!' Farnon breathed thankfully. 'Great work, Mr Meredith—'

'Those gunmen are still somewhere around,' Bart broke in. 'We've dodged 'em so far, but . . .'

The whang of a bullet cut him short and it was followed by several more. Meredith's hat went flying and he picked it up again quickly, holding the crown towards the moon.

'Mmm – two ventilation holes now,' he commented.

'They're closing in on us,' Bart said quickly. He swept the girl up into the saddle of his mare. 'Better get moving!'

They wasted no more time, and in mounting only just missed several shots aimed directly at them. The uncertain light was the one thing that saved them. At last, when they had left the mountain trail behind and once more reached the protection of the more wooded areas, they felt they could breathe again.

'I don't know how you managed it, but thank God you did,' Jane exclaimed, as Bart urged the mare onwards, one arm supporting the girl about the waist.

'Dad's idea entirely,' he explained.

'Yes, but *you* came after me – that's the wonderful thing! After the way you behaved in the Painted Lady I thought—'

'I was tight,' Bart said frankly. 'An unforgivable lapse but I want you to believe me when I say I'll never get tight again.'

He said no more as Meredith and the girl's stepfather caught up. They emerged from the gloomy shadows of the cedar and juniper and began to increase their speed along the arroyo leading to the open pastures below.

'At least we have discovered where these gunmen reside in the mountains – and with their hide-out discovered they'll get out quickly.'

'Right,' Mike Farnon admitted, 'but they'll still have to stay in the mountains. All they can do is change caves and keep a sharper look-out in future. I reckon they won't be taken by surprise a second time.'

'Did you get a close look at any of these men, Dad?' Bart asked.

'No, unfortunately. The firelight wasn't strong enough.'

For a while the ride continued in silence, then Farnon asked:

'Does findin' where these critters is hidin' make any difference to that scheme you had in mind?'

'None at all,' Bart replied, grimly. 'The scheme Dad and I had worked out still holds good – and we'll put it into action at the earliest moment. But before then I'm going to find out what Don Saunders thought he was doing by mauling you, Jane.'

He felt her give a little start against him.

'Surely you don't mean you're going to tackle him face to face?'

'That's just what I do mean!'

'That's the sort of talk I've been waiting to hear,' Jane murmured.

6

FORCED APOLOGY

Jane found that after breakfast the following morning Bart's determination to have a showdown with Don Saunders had not in any way weakened. She reflected that in some way Bart was definitely different, looking at him as he leaned against the rail of the corral enjoying the sunlight and smoking an after-breakfast cigarette.

That slight air of dissipation had vanished. Instead his jaw was lean and tight: there was a hard glitter in his dark-blue eyes. He looked more like a Westerner than he had ever done since arriving in Mountain Peak.

'I'm just not scared any more,' Bart told her, nodding to his father as he joined them. 'I've seen enough of these cut-throats around here to realize that they're all bullies with very little brains. Between us we ought to whip 'em.'

'So you're going ahead again with your plan to try and replace two of their gang?'

'Tonight – but after I've had a word with Don Saunders. And I shan't need a bracer this time, either . . . Meantime,' Brad added, pondering, 'doesn't it strike you as odd, the ease with which we got away with rescuing you last night?'

Meredith held up his perforated Homburg and

regarded it morosely. 'Easy, son?'

'We were shot at, yes – but the shots went wide. And I'm wondering why we weren't pursued more thoroughly. Those triggermen must know the mountains backwards, yet they let us get away with it.'

'Don't forget that they didn't know how many of us were assembled on the trail,' Meredith commented. 'They may have suspected an ambush, and rather than be drawn into it they let us get away . . . Just the same, Miss Jane, I would suggest that you keep a careful watch on yourself in future. They may try and kidnap you again, and next time it might prove a much harder job to rescue you.'

'I know it,' she admitted. 'I'll be careful – never fear.'

With that the subject was dropped, and throughout the day as he helped the girl or her stepfather to do various jobs about the ranch, Bart seemed to be doing a good deal of thinking. It was so marked at the evening meal that Mike Farnon could not help questioning him about it.

'I'm just planning what I'll do to Don Saunders,' Bart explained. 'When I see him later this evening.'

'You sure about tacklin' him?' the big rancher asked dubiously. 'You realize that he's quicker on the draw than any other—'

'I know, and I'm going to risk that. Besides, I want to give Saunders a pretty good look over. I've been remembering about you saying that he might be at the back of the terrorists.'

'I still think that, though I admit I haven't anythin' to show but what Saunders is a straight-shooter – even if he does get a bit tough at times, as he did with Jane last night. She told me what happened,' Farnon added.

'I'm pretty sure Saunders may be at the back of things because I don't see how anybody else *but* him could have known that Jane would be riding home with Dad last night,' Bart said. 'Further, he had good reason for wanting to take care of both Dad and Jane. It would have been easy for him to tip off some of his boys in the saloon to waylay them, and then send a note to you making their demand.'

'Possible I suppose,' Jane agreed. 'But how to prove it?'

'There's that broken gun belt,' he reminded her. 'As far as I've noticed, Saunders doesn't have one – broken, I mean – but probably he realizes it's pretty conspicuous and keeps it hidden until needed. Or he may even borrow or steal it from somebody else every time, so as to get suspicion thrown on that person if at any time things get too hot.'

Mike Farnon fondled his jaw thoughtfully but he did not pass any comment.

'I'm hoping I might get a chance to search his office,' Bart went on, 'and if I draw a blank I might try his ranch house later on. Just see how things go.'

Bart got to his feet resolutely and Meredith did likewise. He looked at the girl and then her stepfather.

'Expect us back when you see us,' he said. 'We're going off on our mission tonight after dealing with Don Saunders, and where it will lead us, Lord knows.'

'Best of luck,' Farnon said quietly. 'I wish I were a younger man: I'd be right beside you.'

Jane accompanied the two men as far as the porch. As Bart climbed into the saddle, she gripped his hand. 'I've packed your saddlebags with provisions,' she said quietly. 'In case you're away some time.'

'Good girl.' Bart stooped down and kissed her upturned face in the twilight.

'Come back safely,' she whispered.

Together the two men cantered their horses out of the yard and to the trail beyond. In fifteen minutes of steady riding they reached the kerosene-lighted high street of

Mountain Peak, dismounting when they gained the noisy regions of the Painted Lady.

Bart patted his twin guns and then strode up the steps into the saloon, his father coming up behind him, one hand resting lightly on his right-hand .38. The same garish, rowdy, tobacco-fumed atmosphere met the pair violently.

A cowpuncher or two glanced, then back again. Grins began to appear, chiefly at the vision of Meredith. His moonlike face remained impassive.

'If it ain't the dude and his Homburg-hatted lapdog again,' a puncher commented – the same man they'd tangled with the previous night.

'You still finding things amusing around here?' Bart asked, striding over to him. 'Last night I wasn't in the mood to argue – but I am now. Get on your feet!'

'Huh?' the puncher questioned blankly.

Abruptly Bart's hand flashed out and tugged the puncher's ten-gallon hat down so that it obscured his vision. Then he hooked his foot under the man's chair and jerked. It crashed over backward, taking the man with it. He struggled savagely and freed his face to find himself looking up into Bart's levelled .45.

'Be warned,' Bart said. 'Any more funny remarks about us and I'll wing you. That clear?'

Nobody spoke. Bart waited a moment, tightened his lips, then returned his gun to its holster. Deliberately he turned his back on the cursing cowpuncher and strode across the saloon to where Don Saunders was standing against one of the pillars. There was a sardonic grin on his handsome face as Bart came up.

'The stranger in town's findin' himself, huh?' he asked drily, returning his cheroot to his teeth.

'Not finding – found,' Bart retorted. 'And I want a word with you, Saunders.'

'Sure. Have a drink?'

'No thanks. I'd quite enough last night . . .' Bart's gaze strayed to Saunders' perfectly normal gun belt, then back to the still grimly smiling face. 'I want an apology for the way you mauled Jane Talbot last night.'

'Listen, stranger.' Saunders grinned more widely than ever. 'I've never apologized to anybody in my life . . . and I don't aim to start with an Eastern dude.'

'I think you'd better do as my son suggests,' Meredith remarked. 'At the moment his mood is decidedly danger-ous.'

'Him? Dangerous?' Saunders spat accurately into the nearest cuspidor. 'Don't make me laugh! Anyways, if I apologized to anybody it would be Jane – and she don't need it. No woman does. They expect to be handled with plenty of vigour around here. Better get movin', stranger,' he finished curtly, whipping out his gun. 'Both you and this pot-bellied coyote you lug around with you.'

Bart's eyes lowered to the gun and then rose again to Saunders' grim features.

'I'll go when I'm ready,' he stated calmly, hooking his thumbs on his pants' belt. 'I'm waiting for that apology first.'

'You're loco! I'll give you ten seconds to get out, then—'

'You'll not shoot,' Bart interrupted. 'You're surrounded here by witnesses. You'd not risk cold-blooded murder to that extent even if you are a power in the town.'

Surprisingly, Saunders relaxed and gave a rueful smile as he reholstered his gun.

'You know, there's somethin' about you two I kinda admire,' he mused. 'You just calmly stand and talk – plain dumb in the face of danger. So you won't move and I won't apologize. Where does that get us?'

'I'll show you,' Bart answered. 'Here, Dad, take my guns.'

Meredith gave the slightest of starts but did as he was bid, pushing the .45s' muzzles down in his pants' belt.

'And Saunders',' Bart added. He looked at the man's suspicious face. 'I've handed over my guns. What's to stop you doing likewise?'

Saunders hesitated. 'What's to stop your father from blowin' the daylights out of me if I hand over my hardware?'

'As I told you before, too many witnesses. And my father is a man of honour. He won't shoot. What I want to do, Saunders, is thrash you into making an apology since it seems that nothing else will do it.'

Saunders' smile returned again. He removed his cheroot, stamped on it, and then handed over his gun, but not to Meredith. He gave it instead to a watching cowpuncher at a nearby table. Then he took off his immaculate, long-tailed black coat. Since he had no jacket to remove Bart rolled up his sleeves and revealed a surprising development of forearm.

Suddenly Bart lashed out a right feint. Saunders jerked his head sideways needlessly – straight into a hammer blow from Bart's left. It jolted him badly, and brought a sudden trickle of blood from one nostril.

Saunders' smile vanished, replaced by hate.

'So you want to play rough . . .'

His massive right bunched and shot straight to Bart's jaw. To the split second Bart dodged it, stood his ground, and retaliated with an uppercut behind which was all the strength his arm possessed. In his day Bart had been the champion wrestler of his college, as well as a passably good boxer. Saunders took the impact on the jaw, slewed round, and half-fell across the nearest table.

In one mighty leap Bart was on top of him, dragged him round, and rained three smashing left-handers. Breathless, blood-streaked, Saunders slipped off the edge of the table and fell face down on the floor.

Bart looked at him for a moment and then dived for him – which was exactly what Saunders had been waiting for. His back arched abruptly like that of an angry cat while his hands gripped Bart's wrists. Bart found himself somersaulted through the air and he landed hard against the plaster and plywood wall, his heavy boots crashing half through it.

Saunders staggered up and drew back his foot savagely, aiming a kick at Bart's head – only it never landed. Bart saw it coming and grabbed it in taut fingers, twisting it violently as he did so. Saunders gave a howl of anguish as he felt his ankle being wrenched out of joint; then unable to keep his balance on one leg he toppled over on top of Bart, his iron-strong hands gripping his throat.

By this time it seemed that everybody in the saloon had gathered into a watching circle. Completely engrossed in this unusual spectacle, nobody said anything to encourage either side.

Bart realized sickly what that grip on his throat implied. He struck back whilst he had strength left. Wrenching his right foot free of the wall panelling he brought up his knee with jolting force, straight into Saunders' stomach. He gasped painfully and his hold loosened.

A violent shove and Bart found the grip had gone and he was on top of the saloon owner. He pinned him there, one knee on his throat and the other on his left arm, nailing him down. Taking his right hand Bart began to turn it with remorseless slowness at the wrist bone.

'Up to you, Saunders,' he panted. 'This is a Judo grip I

learned at college. It'll break your wrist and your arm if it goes far enough.'

Saunders struggled and writhed with savage violence but the triple grip was immovable. Perspiration started into beads on his face as the anguishing twist on his arm gradually intensified.

'I'll kill you for – *hell*!' Saunders broke off, as Bart gave the wrist an extra keen turn.

'That's for the insults,' Bart explained. 'Start apologizing, Saunders – for the way you treated Jane and the things you've said to me . . .'

Saunders shouted an obscenity, then glared upwards at the onlookers.

'You blasted mugs!' he gasped. 'Drag this guy off, can't you?'

The cowpuncher who had taken Saunders' guns moved forward quickly, his intention apparently being to force Bart away at the revolver point, but Meredith suddenly tapped him on the shoulder. The man turned, scowling, and at the same instant Meredith's killing right pistoned into the man's jaw. His knees gave way, and he dropped like a sack of wet flour.

'My apologies,' Meredith murmured, raising and lowering his Homburg. 'Carry on, son,' he added to Bart, and then glanced about him in surprise at the sudden laughter that arose. Nothing so comical, or so devastating, had ever been seen before in the saloon.

'Come on, blast you – apologize!' Bart snapped, and twisted the wrist with double pressure. In spite of himself Saunders yelped at the tearing agony.

'OK, you win!' he gasped. 'I apologize . . . to Jane. I let myself get outa hand . . .'

'And to me and my father. Take it back what you said!'

'I take it back. For God's sake, you're breakin' my arm!'

Bart abruptly removed his grip and stood up. Then he hauled the saloon-owner to his feet, pinning him by his waistcoat front.

Saunders breathed hard as he struggled to recover. Meredith's gaze dropped to a folded square of paper that had fallen from the saloon keeper's pocket. Casually he put his foot upon it and then looked up innocently towards the ceiling.

'OK, so you've got away with it this time,' Saunders breathed, his eyes glinting as Bart took his guns back from his father. 'You and me'll settle this some other time, dude. No guy ever got the better of me for long.'

'First time for everything,' Bart said. Then, the instant Saunders had taken his gun back from the cowpuncher, Bart levelled his .45. 'Take me to your office,' he ordered.

Too late to use his own gun, Saunders hesitated. He wiped a streak of blood from his face.

'What the devil for?'

'A little private chat. And be quick!' Bart added curtly.

Saunders shrugged, then led the way to his office.

Bart followed him. Meredith unostentatiously picked up the fallen note and put it in his pocket, then he followed the two men through the somewhat dazed throng. The office was at the top of a flight of stairs overlooking the saloon itself. Saunders unlocked the door, flung it open, and motioned inside.

Once the oil-lamp had been lighted and the door closed Bart put away his gun and considered the obviously puzzled saloon-owner thoughtfully. Then he jerked his head at Meredith.

'Take a look, Dad,' he ordered. 'See if it's anywhere about.'

'If *what* is?' Saunders snapped.

'You'll soon know if we find it,' Bart answered. 'And it'll

mean plenty of trouble for you. If we don't . . . Well, I may have made a mistake.'

Saunders sighed, and then slumped thankfully into the swivel-chair beside his roll-top desk. He lighted a fresh cheroot then watched in puzzlement as Meredith prowled about the room, opening and shutting every drawer. Eventually he shook his head and looked at Bart.

'Nothing here, son.'

'Open your safe, Saunders,' Bart ordered, his gun coming into his hand.

Saunders glared. 'Why the hell should I? I've private papers in there, and I—'

'*Get it open!*' Bart roared. 'I'm not interested in any damned papers. I'm looking for something else.'

Saunders shrugged, and getting up he went over to the safe, fishing in his pocket for the key. He pulled open the safe's heavy door.

'You might do the hell of a lot better if you came clean as to what the hell you're looking for . . .'

Bart examined inside the safe, and satisfied himself that the gun belt was not there. He straightened and glanced at Saunders who was looking as puzzled as he was angry.

'All right,' he said, holstering his gun. 'Seems I was wrong. See you again sometime, Saunders – and go easy on the way you talk and act in future. Come on, Dad.'

Saunders watched them leave and then scratched the back of his neck. 'Damned if I get it,' he mused, drawing on his cheroot. 'Those two act like they're loco.' Then he gave a faint grin that might have been admiration.

When he and his father had passed through the saloon – and been given plenty of room in the process – and reached the boardwalk outside Bart paused and cuffed up his hat. He grinned in the kerosene light.

'In the local idiom, Dad, how am I doin'?'

'Magnificently, son. I'm sure Miss Jane will be proud of you, when she learns of what's happened – as she will. You'll be the talk of the town.'

Bart shrugged. 'Pity we didn't find that gun belt, though. Only thing to do now is carry out our original plan and look for a suitable spot to hide whilst we wait for the next raid. We know their HQ is somewhere in the hills, and that means there's only one trail they can follow from that direction.'

As they stepped down from the boardwalk, Meredith raised a hand as a thought suddenly struck him.

'Wait! During your fight a paper fell from Saunders' pocket and I – er – snitched it. I haven't had time to look at it yet.'

Frowning to himself Bart took the folded piece of paper his father gave him and peered at it in the light of the streetlamps.

'Looks like a ladder.' Bart shrugged. 'Take a look at it.'

Meredith did so and found himself studying a rough ink-drawn plan of the district. The mountains were plainly marked, and here and there were crosses that were probably intended to indicate the holdings of the various rancher-owners. The ladder to which Bart had referred went from north to south of the drawing – two straight parallel lines with rungs at quarter-inch intervals. The whole thing was very roughly done and, as such, utterly incomprehensible.

'Most peculiar, son,' Meredith commented at last, thinking: I'm sure it ought to suggest something significant, but I can't see it at the moment.

'We'll keep it, anyway,' Bart decided, putting the paper in his shirt pocket. 'Now let's be on our way.'

They unhitched their horses, mounted them, and

started off up the high street. As they went a horseman riding in from the opposite end of the street watched them go. He dismounted and secured his mare to the Painted Lady's tie rail.

'Wonder if he managed to give Don Saunders the beatin' he figured?' Mike Farnon mused. 'I surely hope so!'

With a grim expression on his rugged face he pushed through the batwings into the saloon. Immediately several of the men assembled at the tables nodded to him familiarly. He spoke to one or two of them, wandering in and out of the tables, and finally asked a question of Saunders' closest cohort – the man who had held his gun during the fight.

'Where *is* Don tonight?' Farnon asked, looking about him. 'I want a word with him.'

The puncher grinned. 'Last we saw of him he went to his office with the dude and his father. And between you an' me Don sure took a beatin'!'

'You mean Bart Meredith actually beat the hide off him?'

'Mighty near it . . .' The puncher reflected. 'Those guys are livin' with you, ain't they? Where in heck do they come from an' why?'

'It's a long story,' Farnon answered. 'Right now I need to find Don. See you again.'

He turned and made his way amidst the tables to the staircase leading to Saunders' office. When he knocked on the door the saloon-owner's gruff voice bade him enter. Farnon did so and stood and eyed Saunders as he lolled at his roll-top desk dabbing at his nose with his handkerchief.

'So it's you, Mike. What's on your mind?'

Mike Farnon smiled faintly as he contemplated the

bruises on Saunders' features Then his gaze dropped to the bloodstains on the handkerchief.

'All right, laugh!' Saunders snapped, glaring. 'So I got myself beaten up by a blasted dude!'

'I'm laughin' all right,' Farnon conceded. 'Anythin' that makes you uncomfortable, Don, is OK by me. How does it feel to have an Easterner beat the daylights out of you?'

'Actually, I'm not beefin' about it. I was mistaken in that jigger. I'd sized him up as an all-time tenderfoot; now I know different.' Saunders put his handkerchief away and narrowed his eyes. 'Anyway, what the hell d'you want?'

'I came to ask for more time to pay up what I owe you.'

Saunders scowled. 'Depends how long. You oughta have sense enough to know that you shouldn't gamble without the backin' to pay for your debts if you lose. You're still owin' me pretty nearly eight thousand dollars, and I'm getting' tired of waitin' for it.'

'You can stand it. You're the richest man hereabouts.'

'That ain't the point. I'm not one to let you squirm out of your obligations.'

'Not a case of that, Don. Eight thousand dollars aren't so easy to find these days and—'

'You've good cattle and good trade,' Saunders interrupted. 'Get that money inside a week, Mike, or I'll take cattle to the value of what you owe me whether you like it or not. If you were as square as some people think I'd give you every chance, but I don't think you are. And I never did think so!'

Mike Farnon's expression changed. 'What do you mean?'

'I mean that I haven't forgotten how some time ago you were nearly run out of town for cattle rustling, then you fixed it so's to make yourself look innocent.'

'I *was* innocent!' Farnon declared angrily 'I never rustled a steer in my life!'

'OK, that's your story. I figure that you've a crooked streak some place and for that reason I'm puttin' the screws down about my money. You've a week, Mike – no longer.'

'You'll get it!' Farnon retorted. 'Yes, you'll get it!'

The door slammed as he went out.

7

COUNTER ATTACK

IT was well past midnight when Bart and his father left the pastureland behind and reached the mountain foothills. They were considerably ahead of the moonrise, and with only dim starlight were unlikely to be picked out by a gunman.

'You know, son,' Meredith remarked, as they jogged along the arroyo trail, 'I think we've left behind us a world to which we will never return.'

'You mean Mountain Peak?'

'No – Boston. Look at all this.' Meredith waved his arm. 'Where is there anything even comparable with it back home? Look at these mountains and the stars; smell the air. I never knew I was alive at all until we came out here.'

'But you've your successful import business back in Boston,' Bart pointed out. 'I know your partner is looking after it for you whilst we're out here, but . . .'

Meredith smiled. 'If we come out of all this in one piece, I'm seriously thinking of selling him my controlling interest in the business, and settling here in Arizona. What do you think of the idea?'

'You should make enough from the sale to be able to

settle just about anywhere,' Bart said. Then for a while he fell to thought as the horses ambled on. 'Come to think of it,' he added, 'I haven't any real need to go back to Boston either. With the allowance Mother left to my credit I could spend the rest of my days out here and draw money from the bank every month as I needed it.'

'That wouldn't satisfy you, son – not now. I think you would much prefer to work.'

'You're darned right I would. Confidentially, I'd like to marry Jane, if she'd have me and then buy a ranch some-where and settle on it. Maybe rebuild Dave's place. Naturally I'd expect you to stay with us.'

Meredith smiled. 'An interesting prospect. But before any of that can come about, this terrorism has to be smashed. Miss Jane expects it of you, and I don't think she will ever agree to marry you until this valley is a safe place to live.'

The journey up the arroyo continued in silence. Then, when they had reached the point where the junipers and cedars flourished, the trail passing unmistakably from the mountains through the midst of the trees, Meredith spoke again.

'I suggest we should camp here. Any outlaws coming to the valley will be forced to come this way, and we have the advantage of cave and rock cover – and also low tree branches, from which we might do quite a deal.'

They took the reins and led the horses, until they had found a respectable-sized natural cave gaping in the mountain face. Securing the animals to a rock projection they removed the provisions from the saddlebags and then set about the task of equipping their temporary home.

Meredith set out a rough meal of canned food upon a thin sheet of mackintosh, then turned to preparing some coffee on a small spirit-stove. At length he and Bart settled down to an alfresco meal for which they were more than ready.

'I've been thinking about that note we found on Saunders,' Bart frowned. 'But that ladder business still doesn't make sense to me.'

'Same here, son. As regards Saunders himself having some connection with the gang, as you seem to think, where's his motive? He's already one of the richest men in the district . . .'

'So what? Remember the old saying – much would have more! He owns that saloon; he has a big cattle ranch, but as I understand in these parts a ranch is never really big enough,' Bart went on. 'If you have no particular scruples there's one sure way to expand – chase out those already on the land because they'd never sell in the ordinary way. It's the only life they know.'

'So you reckon that if Saunders scared away the land-holders he might grab the land himself and become a virtual dictator in the town?'

'It's possible,' Bart insisted. 'If he isn't responsible for the terrorists, then who is? There must be a mastermind at the head of them – somebody who knows the district pretty well. So I think we can discount an outsider being involved.'

'But not entirely,' Meredith mused. 'Suppose someone who once lived here was outlawed, and has a grudge that is leading him to take revenge in the form of these raids? We might get a lead by asking the sheriff later if anybody was run out of town before we came here. But in the meantime, our best bet is to hope that some kind of raid will be attempted tonight, so we can make our move.'

Thereafter they took it in turns to keep watch – but nothing disturbed the peacefulness. Bart had the last watch before dawn. He sat in the cave mouth watching the early light appear, visible through the interlacing of foliage in the treetops. It began with the sky becoming molten gold, turning the dim, squatting buttresses of the distant peaks into sharp, blackly cut spires and domes. Then, presently, the vermilion feathers appeared, creeping out of nowhere into the deepening blue as the first rays of the new day struck upwards.

Far in the distance, where lay the desert and wilderness the grey mists dissolved into purple and poured upwards, to vanish as though they had never been. Swiftly, imperceptibly, the night gave place to the pouring effulgence of the sun.

Bart took his eyes from the scene at last and turned to awaken his father. As he prepared the breakfast – once again coffee and canned provisions – he brooded in some disgust over the fact that nothing untoward had occurred.

Breakfast was consumed without anything disturbing the peace, and it was a peace that remained throughout the long day. Eventually the day passed into a second night.

Bart elected to do the first watch while his father snoozed. Ten o'clock came and went. Eleven. Then just after midnight Bart, half dozing himself, suddenly tautened. A faint reverberation was growing steadily louder. Bart reached over and shook his father into wakefulness. Instantly he heaved to his feet.

'Time for action, son,' he said abruptly. 'There's a party of horsemen descending from the mountains and we're getting their vibrations. They're still some distance away and that gives us time to act. Follow me!'

Meredith paused only long enough to take the lariats from the saddle horns of the horses, then he hurried out of the cave into the wooded region outside. In the dim starlight he indicated the ancient arroyo that ran through the midst of the trees.

'They'll have to come this way and pass under these thickly foliaged overhanging trees,' he explained. 'We'll be waiting in the trees. They can't move quickly in this confined spot, which will give us enough time to select the two men we want to drop our ropes over. You should be able to get someone who approximates to you in build easily enough. Not so easy for me – just have to hope for the best.'

'You make it sound easy, Dad,' said Bart, 'but what is to stop the others noticing what's going on?'

Meredith glanced about him. 'We can hardly see each other in this dim light, and we are not yet in the full shadow of the trees. It will take us all our time to see the men who pass beneath us, but being only about a yard above their heads we ought to be able to judge their dimensions . . .'

Meredith broke off and moved urgently as the sound of the approaching riders, moving warily now down the mountain declivity, became louder. In the space of a few minutes he and Bart had selected the most massive low-hanging branch they could find overreaching the trail, and upon it they remained, their lariats ready, the foliage hiding everything except their watching eyes.

In all there were about a dozen riders, their mounts picking their way slowly amongst the loose stones and moving between the closely spaced trees. Motionless, intent, the two men watched, studying the passing men beneath them as best they could.

Meredith acted suddenly, selecting the largest man in the party. The outlaw had no chance to cry out, for the noose dropped over his neck and tightened so fiercely that he could hardly breathe. He was dragged silently from his horse, threshing frantically as Meredith lowered him just sufficiently for his feet to touch the ground.

'Quick, son,' Meredith urged, as the party moved on. 'Take out that last man. Hurry!'

Bart flung his rope. The noose landed over the last rider's shoulders, tightened, and, supporting himself with his knee braced on the tree-branch, Bart jerked the man backwards. Immediately, as he hit the ground, the noose slid up from his shoulders and tightened about his neck. Fiercely, Bart dragged him to a halt whilst the rest of the party went on its way steadily through the dense trees, unaware as yet that two of their members were missing.

Meredith dropped to the ground and lumbered after the two aimlessly wandering horses the two men had been using. He caught their reins, brought them back and tied them to a nearby tree. Then Bart came beside him and, guns drawn, they removed the ropes from the two men they had snatched. In another moment their weapons had been tossed away into the undergrowth.

'Move!' Bart ordered curtly. 'Into that cave there!'

Half-strangled and with the guns trained upon them neither of the outlaws put up any argument. They stumbled forward and into the cave, then Brad snatched down the kerchiefs which were still up to their eyes. There was a sputtering flare as Meredith struck a match, then Bart gave a little gasp. Though he had never seen the big man before the other one, whom he had singled out for himself, was immediately familiar. It was the cowpuncher with the scarred face.

'Couldn't have taken anybody better!' Bart murmured. 'All right, start talking. Where's the raid to be tonight?'

'Go to hell!' the big fellow commented sourly – then he recoiled as Bart delivered a powerful slap across his face.

'*Where's the raid to be?* I'll wing you if you don't speak – and you'd better believe it!'

The big fellow still remained silent but the scarred man spoke instead.

'The information won't do you any good far as I can see,' he said. 'We'd figured on raidin' the Slanting F – an' that's just what the boys will do, with us or without us.'

'The Slanting F!' Bart gasped. 'Mike Farnon's place?'

'Yeah. Reckon it's time him and that gal of his was taken care of. They've got off lightly so far.'

'Let's go,' Bart snapped, swinging round, but his father caught his arm.

'First we've got to exchange shirts – these men are wearing check shirts and we are not. Our pants will do since they are riding-pants, same as theirs are. Then we need to tie them up and gag them until we return . . .'

'All right, all right, but we've got to hurry!' Bart urged, and ripped open the front of his shirt.

Inside five minutes the change-over was complete and Bart and his father had their kerchiefs in position over their faces. They left the two outlaws shirtless, securely bound and gagged, and then leapt swiftly to the saddles of the men's horses and began the journey down the mountain trail as fast as safety allowed.

They had reached the pastureland, neither speaking to the other in their urgency, before they caught up with the rest of the party. The onward journey continued steadily under the stars until at length the Slanting F began to loom up in the dim light. On the still night air there came the faint lowing of uneasy cattle. Within a hundred yards of the corral gates the leader of the party called a halt.

Bart and his father drew to a stop also, waiting, quite unrecognizable in the deep gloom.

'I'd like to get hold of that leader and find out who he is,' Bart whispered. 'Or, failing that, take a look at his gun belt.'

'That will have to wait, son. Frankly, I don't like the look of things. Miss Jane and her stepfather are in real danger.'

'You guys back there all know the plan,' the leader called gruffly, his voice unidentifiable to Bart and his father. 'Mike Farnon's outfit will be in town by now, so we'll try and get Farnon and the gal out here afore we burn down the spread. But if they're stubborn they'll have to take their chance. If they start shootin', shoot straight back. Farnon will be a tough customer if he escapes to tell the tale. You fellers stay here: I'll go and see what I can do.'

Bart moved uneasily in his saddle as he watched the leader slide down to the ground and go forward in the starlight to the yard gates.

'What in hell do we do, Dad? We can't let these cut-throats shoot old man Farnon and Jane.'

'Wait to see what happens,' Meredith muttered. 'We'll have to act according to—'

He broke off at the sudden report of the outlaw leader's gun as he fired into the air. Then there came the gleam of an oil-lamp from one of the windows of the ranch house. Then it shifted position and presently reappeared on the porch.

'What the blazes goes on out here?' the voice of Farnon demanded. Dimly visible in the light of the lamp he was holding was Jane, a little to one side of him.

'We've got you covered, Mike,' the outlaw called from the gate. 'Better not try anythin' – nor the gal either. You've ten seconds to clear out afore we set your ranch afire and turn your cattle loose.'

'You blasted skunk!' Mike Farnon roared back. 'What good would it do us? You'd only kill us, same as you've done with the rest of the poor devils in this valley.'

'You've got that right, feller,' the outlaw answered drily.

'You and your gal will be taken out to the desert and left there, bound hand and foot. We'll let the sunlight kill you – and leave no bullets in you for a sheriff to start tryin' to trace.'

'What sort of choice is that?' Farnon shouted. 'Go to hell! We'll take it clean first and make you fire bullets into us so they'll be found inside us later. Now get movin'!' And Farnon's revolver suddenly blazed four times in quick succession.

The outlaw flung himself flat, fired back, and then at a crouching run regained his horse. More bullets came whanging across from the Slanting F's porch and, as well as they could on their pitching horses, the outlaws fired back.

'Extraordinary,' Meredith commented, puzzled. 'I'm surprised that experienced gunmen waste their time trying to pick off each other in the dark unless Farnon's hoping the sound of his shots may arouse some of the other ranchers about here in the hope they might come to his rescue . . .'

'What the hell are you mugs waitin' for?' the outlaw leader bellowed. 'Get the darned place fired. Lefty, where's that torch of yourn?'

There was an abrupt flaring of light amidst the crossfire as a torch blazed. Flung by the hand of Lefty it sailed through the air and landed near the Slanting F, several feet short.

'Again!' the outlaw yelled. 'Another. All you've got!'

'Wait here, son,' Meredith murmured to Bart. 'Something I have to do . . .'

Before Bart could speak his father had gone. He goaded his horse swiftly round the rear of the wildly shooting group of outlaws and so gained the gates of the corral. He dismounted swiftly, flung the gates open, fired twice –

which shots were never noticed amidst the general exchange – and then watched the result. It was as he had anticipated. Startled, the herd began to move, stampeded in fact, straight towards the group of outlaws under the stars.

Grinning to himself Meredith swung back into his saddle and raced his horse round at top speed to where he had left Bart.

'What the devil have you done, Dad?' Bart panted, pitching up and down.

'You'll see! Right now we must get out of the way,' Meredith responded, spurring his horse forward. 'Follow me!'

Belatedly, the rest of the outlaw group had now seen the danger. There was some 500 head of cattle in the corral and to stand in their track, startled as they were, was sheer suicide. The men broke up, scattered, and went racing away in various directions under the stars, the blindly hurtling steers pursuing them.

'Nice work, Dad,' Bart commented. 'But how do we ever catch up with those men again and start trying to find out which one is which? They're utterly scattered. They'll return to their headquarters by separate routes. We've lost our chance of finding out who the leader is!'

'It was that or the destruction of the Slanting F and the death of Farnon and Miss Jane. I had to act to save them. As for us,' Meredith added, as Farnon and the girl became visible racing across the yard in an effort to stop the cattle, 'we'd better get away. We might find it hard to convince Farnon that we aren't part of the gang, even if Miss Jane knows what we're up to.'

He wheeled his horse round and Bart followed suit. Swiftly, bearing ever further away from the demoralized gunmen and the steers racing after them, they rode away across the pastureland, turning presently in a wide arc so as to bring themselves once more in line with the mountain foothills.

'This has been pretty much of a wash-out,' Bart said, somewhat bitterly. 'We saved the ranch, and Jane and Mike, but what have we personally got out of it? Nothing! We'll have to start all over again next time there's a raid, granting there is one after those outlaws have had such a beating.'

'They'll be back all right,' Meredith answered quietly. 'And I'd hardly call the time wasted. Don't forget we've got two very useful hostages back at the cave.'

'You don't expect to get anything out of them, surely?'

'There are ways, son. And we know that the scarred-faced man frequents the Painted Lady and is therefore a native of the town. Probably he knows quite well who the leader of the terrorists is.'

Bart said nothing as they sped on under the night sky with the thunder of earth beneath the horses' hoofs. Then Meredith resumed:

'We've also been lucky as far as those two men are concerned. In the stampede all the members of the gang were separated. If two of them do not return those remaining will not worry unduly. You realize that we cannot allow those two men to return to the fold and say we attacked them and took their places.'

'I'd forgotten all about them in the general urgency,' Bart admitted. 'We can't shoot them out of hand, Dad. I draw the line at that.'

'So do I, son. My original idea was to keep them prisoners in the cave until we had succeeded in rounding up the whole gang, but the way things have gone, we'll just have to try and get the truth out of them and then take them to the sheriff for him to deal with.'

'I guess there's nothing else for it,' Bart admitted; then they both gave up talking as they reached the mountain foothills.

8

MOUNTAIN DEATH

The two began the long, ticklish ascent up the arroyo that led to the region of trees where their cave was situated. They moved as rapidly as possible for the moon was beginning to show signs of rising. In half an hour their journey was finished and they began to breathe more freely as they left the open spaces behind and the horses picked their way amidst the trees and bubbling, half-hidden streams.

'Watch it, son,' Meredith cautioned, drawing his gun. 'One or other of those triggermen may have passed this way and discovered something about our cave.'

Accordingly they approached the cave cautiously, but found it exactly as they had left it, with the two bound gangsters still inside, their backs against the wall.

Though it left little room Meredith brought in the two extra horses and tethered them at the back of the cave. Then, stooping, he removed the gag from the mouth of each man in turn.

'It's time you two did a little talking . . .' Meredith threw down the Stetson he had borrowed from the big fellow and stood waiting.

'You've some hopes, Homburg,' Scarred Cheek growled.

'I want to know who your leader is – not the leader of the few cheap terrorists we routed tonight, but the mastermind behind the whole series of raids. Though you may not know what their purpose is, I am sure you must know who is back of everything.'

There was a long silence, then the puncher said slowly:

'I reckon I've only one answer for you, Homburg, an' that dude son of yours, an' it's this . . .'

At blurring speed his hands unexpectedly came from behind him and seized on Meredith's throat with strangling pressure. The savage attack was so unexpected he was on the ground before he knew it. Bart's hand whipped down to his gun but he was not quick enough. A blow in the face from the second man struck him like exploding fire and he hurtled backwards into the wall of the cave.

Immediately he sprang himself forward and seized the big man round the neck. A blow in the stomach jolted him; another in the jaw swung him away – then he twisted and lashed out a savage right-hander that caught the big man in the face. He stumbled backwards and fell down at the rear of the cave amidst an uneasy stirring of the horses' hoofs.

Bart crouched, breathing hard, aware that his father also was struggling savagely with the man on the floor. Then the man at the back of the cave catapulted forward. Bart waited until the last second, then dodged aside, delivering a killing blow on the back of the man's neck at the same instant. He went stumbling out of the cave-opening and crashed amidst the rocks outside.

Immediately Bart was after him, dragged him up and aimed blow after blow, jerking back once or twice as he received savage backhanders. Then his right and left shot out with pistonlike impact, keeling the man backwards. He stumbled helplessly amidst the rocks, made a frantic effort to save himself, and then vanished with a wailing cry that floated into silence and was gone.

Bart moved forward slowly and pulled up sharp when he came to the spot where the man had disappeared. He was looking into the deep gorge that ran alongside the trail.

'None of my doing,' Bart muttered. 'He started it . . .' He hurried back to the cave, only just in time to prevent the remaining puncher from delivering a stunning right-hander upon the struggling Meredith.

'On your feet!' Bart ordered, sticking the barrel of his gun in the man's back. 'Quick!'

The man obeyed, panting, his hands slightly raised.

'Thanks, son,' Meredith gasped, getting to his feet and batting the dust from his clothes. 'He caught me at a disadvantage.' He stooped, picked up his hat and put it on. 'You OK?'

'I'm all right, but the big guy went over the trail edge into the chasm.'

'Which makes you a murderer!' Scarred Cheek snapped.

'Murder shouldn't worry you: you're an expert. Anyway, it was self-defence . . .'

'I presume,' Meredith looked at the puncher, 'that you two got loose by rubbing your ropes through on the rock edges?'

'Right,' the man agreed sourly. 'Unfortunately we'd only just managed it when you two came back. What do you figure on doin' now?' he demanded. 'I ain't talkin', either. Do what you the hell you like!'

'I might try my judo grip on him,' Bart reflected, turning to look at his father. 'It did the trick with Saunders.

What do you think?'

'I had thought of . . .' Meredith began, then he broke off and made a dive at the puncher as, suddenly dropping his right hand, the man lashed at Bart's gun, gripped it, and whirled it into his fingers.

'Get your mitts up, both of you!' the puncher breathed, levelling the weapon.

Slowly the two men obeyed and a faint grin came to the man's face in the dimly reflected starlight.

'When you've got a bead on a guy, dude, keep it there! You lookin' at Homburg here was just what I was waitin' for. OK, gimme my shirt back. It's blasted cold without it and there's somethin' in the pocket I'd kinda like to keep.'

Bart gave a start and then compressed his lips. It had never occurred to him to look in the pocket of the borrowed shirt.

'Get it off, damn you!' the puncher yelled, so Bart began to obey.

When he had got half-way through the task, with the shirt waving over his head and his arms still in the sleeves, he suddenly hesitated and seemed to be having difficulty in getting his head free. The puncher watched him narrowly, but even so he was caught unprepared as Bart suddenly brought the enveloping folds of the shirt forward and downward, smothering the puncher's face and swinging aside his gun hand.

Immediately Meredith dived for the weapon and whipped it up. Bart tore free the shirt and delivered a smashing right-hander, which struck the unbalanced cowpuncher in the mouth. With a gasp he toppled sideways – then, helped on his way by a second punch on the jaw, he crashed outside amidst the rocks.

Recovering quickly he lurched to his feet again and

went blundering away down the trail.

'Don't shoot!' Bart ordered his father quickly, as he caught the glint of the gun barrel. 'It'll give away our position. I'll get him.'

He dived out of the cave and raced in pursuit of the fleeing man amidst the thickly clustered trees. Suddenly, with a gasping scream, the cowpuncher jerked to a standstill, swayed, and then fell heavily. At the same time there was a ripping and tearing of branches and a rustling of undergrowth.

Cautiously, Bart moved forward, alert for sudden attack, but nothing happened. The puncher remained motionless, oddly crumpled, face down in the thickly weeded earth. Bart dropped on one knee beside him and turned him over.

Impaled through the puncher's chest, practically on a line with his heart, was a broken branch of spearlike thinness. Evidently it had been jutting out of the undergrowth and in his wild dash forward in the dark the puncher had never seen it. In his fall the end had broken off, leaving the shaft driven almost right through his body.

There came a crackling of undergrowth as Meredith came to investigate. Bart rose from gripping the cowpuncher's wrist.

'Dead,' Bart announced. 'His own fault . . .' And he added the details.

'Search his pants' pockets, and if there is nothing in them we'll dispose of his body in the gorge,' his father said levelly. 'If it remains here and any of the gang see it they may think of looking for us.'

Bart nodded. They made their examination swiftly but did not find anything. So they lifted the limp body between them, carried it to the edge of the trail, and then watched it roll down the rocky slope in the moonlight until it vanished from sight. Meredith raised and lowered his hat briefly.

'Just respect for the dead, son,' he explained, smiling sardonically. 'Though not for him individually. As a member of the gang that killed David, it's merely the settling of an account for us . . . good riddance! Now we'd better see what there was in his shirt pocket which he was so anxious to recover.'

To unbutton the shirt pockets was only a moment's work and in the left-hand one there was a sheet of paper folded into four, dirty on the creases from where it had rubbed against the fabric.

Meredith struck a match and cupped the flame to hide it from the outer world.

'I'll be damned!' Bart muttered, staring at the sheet as he smoothed it out. 'Same thing again, with just a couple of differences!'

The drawing of the valley itself was again in evidence, with the peculiar ladder drawn straight across it. Only this map was a far more thorough job, executed in indian ink, and instead of crosses to mark the various holdings there were the actual names – including that of the Slanting F and the Double Y, which Bart's brother had owned.

'The ladder ends in each case at a city,' Meredith mused. 'Wilson City to the north and Caradoc City to the south. And the ladder between. Once again it would seem as though the shortest distance between two points is a straight line.'

'Shortest distance . . .' Bart repeated slowly. 'I begin to think you may have something there, Dad.' Bart folded up the paper in sudden decision. 'I'm going to play a hunch for all I'm worth. I think we should take a trip to Wilson City by train – and if we don't find what we want there we'll go to Caradoc.'

'Why?'

'You can ask, but I'm not going to answer – chiefly because my hunch may be wrong. Besides, I want to try this angle on my own initiative. Frankly, Dad, up to now you seem to have done most of the thinking!'

'Only for the good of both of us, son. I take it, then, that you intend we abandon these mountains?'

'Yes, because I have a dim suspicion that our answer may lie in one of those two cities. I know we discussed tackling the sheriff in regard to any outlaw who might have been kicked out of town, but that can wait too. I'm not particularly keen on the idea of dragging the law into things just yet.'

'I'll turn the horses loose before we go,' Meredith said. 'Might take too much explaining if we turned up with them at the Slanting F.'

To judge from appearances, as Bart and his father approached the Slanting F in the dawn light, everything was once more under control. The cattle appeared to be safely corralled again and the ranch house was quiet and dark.

The two men stabled their horses and then went across the yard to the porch. Bart fumbled in his pockets for the duplicate key to the screen door which Jane had loaned him, and presently he and his father were inside. They froze at a sudden sharp voice from the living-room.

'Hold it, whoever you are! I got you covered!'

An oil-lamp gleamed into being and Mike Farnon came forward, a Colt in his hand. He stood in the living-room doorway for a moment, and then relaxed.

'I'll be durned! You two! Sorry, fellers.'

There was a sudden movement behind Farnon and Jane, fully dressed, came into view.

'Been a whole heap of trouble around here tonight,' Farnon explained. 'Which is why Jane and me are on the look-out. We thought you were some of them damned terrorists come back.'

Farnon told them what had happened, and finished in a grim voice: 'We beat the critters, though. Got all our cattle back, too – some of our neighbours came out after hearing the shots, and they helped us round them up. Somehow the corral gate must have got open – but it was a good job it did. Them steers saved us, I reckon . . . But come right in,' he broke off. 'Jane, rustle up some coffee and sandwiches. Guess we can all do with it after this night's work.'

Jane nodded and hurried off into the kitchen regions. With a significant glance at his father, Bart led the way into the living-room and threw himself down thankfully in one of the easy-chairs. Meredith did likewise, passing a hand over his semi-bald head and breathing heavily.

'You two seem as though you've been doin' some hard ridin',' Farnon commented.

'We've been trying to get evidence,' Bart replied, 'and I think maybe we've got something. Tell you more about it when Jane comes back. She ought to hear it too.'

She was not very long returning with the coffee and sandwiches; then as the dawn light strengthened swiftly through the windows Bart launched into an explanation, the only thing he suppressed being the information about the second sketch he had found in the cowpuncher's pocket.

'I'll be doggoned!' Farnon declared at last, staring. 'So you actually joined the gang itself? And it was you, Mr Meredith, who opened the corral?'

'At that moment I could think of no other way to save things – and of course we couldn't join you without giving ourselves away to the terrorists.'

'If that don't beat everythin'!' Farnon muttered, shaking his head. 'But you say it hasn't got you far? You still don't know who owns that broken gun belt?'

'No,' Bart admitted. 'But for the moment I'm shelving that problem. I'm taking a trip to Wilson City immediately after breakfast – and if I don't find what I expect I'll go on to Caradoc.'

'Why?' Farnon asked in surprise.

'Maybe a valuable clue to ending this terrorist business,' Bart answered. 'And that's all I feel like saying at the moment.'

'Any reason why I can't come with you?' Jane asked eagerly. 'I've been in on most things so far.' Then as her stepfather looked at her curiously she added, 'I knew all about their intention to join up with the gang, only they thought it best to keep it secret in case anything leaked out.'

'Meanin' that you couldn't trust me to keep quiet?' Farnon asked grimly.

'Well, you do spend quite a lot of time in the Painted Lady,' Jane said, somewhat uncomfortably. 'And had you perhaps been a bit loosened up with whiskey, or something, you might have said too much.'

'I see.' Farnon sighed. 'OK – so you want to go with these two. Guess you're old enough to make your own decisions, gal.'

Bart reflected, then: 'All right, Jane, no reason why you shouldn't come. I'm not expecting any real trouble to begin with.'

'How come, if it's connected with the terrorism?' Farnon queried.

'I said no trouble to *begin* with,' Bart corrected. 'The sparks will soon fly if I get the information on the terrorists I'm hoping for . . .'

He refused to be drawn any further and, the coffee and sandwiches finished, he and his father went for a change and shave. They packed their bags, managed to get in an hour's doze before breakfast; then immediately after it they set off for the station, Jane with them in the smart outfit she had been wearing on the day they had first encountered her on the train. Her stepfather drove the buckboard and team that took them to the station.

His farewell seemed somewhat piqued, as if he didn't approve of being kept in the dark. Even Jane was little the wiser, with Bart refusing to tell her exactly what was in his mind.

'You're just being obstinate,' she declared as she and Bart – his father being asleep in his seat in the first carriage – sat together in the observation car at the rear of the train, contemplating the Arizonan countryside. 'What difference can it make?'

'So far,' Bart smiled, 'every bit of deductive thinking that's gone on has been done by my father. I used to be happy for him to make the decisions, but things have altered now that I have you watching my moves. I just want to see if I can bring this off on my own bat and leave him standing.'

Jane became silent and ceased trying to probe. Bart sat watching the girl as the wind stirred her fair hair about her forehead and the intense sunlight gave remarkable clarity to her features.

'Dad was right in one thing,' Bart said at length, and Jane's blue eyes turned from studying wilderness and desert. 'He said that the more one sees of the West the less one is interested in going back home to Boston.'

'You mean the view from here has made you appreciate that there is something out here worth having? That's

111

odd, ever since we came out here you've had your eyes on me, and scarcely looked at the surroundings!'

'Precisely.' Bart grinned widely.

The girl looked away with a demureness that pleased him. He reached out suddenly and caught her hand.

'Jane, listen to me . . . There isn't any question but what we love each other. What is there to stop us getting married?'

'The terrorists,' she answered quietly.

'How? Even if I married you I'd still hunt for them, and—'

'I don't think you would. If we married now you'd move me out of that terror-ridden valley to a quiet ranch. We'd have to take Dad with us because he's too old to fight for himself. The whole business there would be forgotten. But I don't think it should be allowed to. It was the murder of your brother that started you on the hunt, remember: if only for his memory I think you should finish what you have begun. I was brought up in Mountain Peak Valley. My roots are deep. That is why I want you to destroy the menace hanging over it. Do that . . . then we'll marry.'

Bart flirted his cigarette over the rail and smiled ruefully.

'So Dad was right again! He said you'd never agree to marry me until I'd cleaned up this band of cut-throats.'

The train twisted and turned on its long, roundabout journey through the rocks, sometimes climbing laboriously up a steep gradient, at others plunging through seemingly endless tunnels, all the time following an enormous curve.

'How long does it take to get to Wilson City?' Bart asked, thinking.

'About ten hours. We should be in by nightfall.'

'That long? To cover a distance of about two hundred miles?'

'It just so happens that the railway doesn't take a straight line,' Jane explained.

'And the shortest distance between two points, Miss Jane, is a straight line,' commented Meredith's voice, as he stood in the doorway of the observation car and looked down benignly. 'Pardon my intrusion, son, but the first call for lunch will be in ten minutes. I thought you'd like to know.'

The sun was near setting when at last the train concluded its roundabout journey and drew into the big railroad station at Wilson City. Stiff, and bored with the travelling, the trio alighted, the two men carrying the bags between them.

'Fortunately, I know this place pretty well,' Jane said. 'We should be able to get accommodation at the Pineview Hotel – that's it straight down the main street.'

At the hotel the desk-clerk frowned in doubt at Bart's obviously Eastern accent. Then Jane stepped in and secured their booking in her forthright fashion.

'When we've freshened up and had a meal, what happens?' she asked, as they walked upstairs. 'This is your show, Bart.'

'We're going to take a buckboard tour of the city,' he responded, and the girl and his father regarded him dubiously.

'We didn't come here to sight-see, Bart,' Jane said as they stepped out on the second corridor. 'It's business – isn't it?'

'In this case sight-seeing *is* the business. I'll explain if what I hope comes off.'

After they were rested and refreshed, Bart talked again

to the hotel's desk-clerk and managed to hire someone to drive them around in a buckboard. They settled, somewhat uncomfortably in Meredith's case, and the tour began. Not knowing what they were supposed to look for, Meredith and Jane contented themselves with merely surveying – and found it interesting in that Wilson City was a highly organized and up-to-date town . . . From the high streets they passed into the quieter regions, failed to discover what Bart was looking for, and so gradually – under his directions – the elderly driver came back to the city centre. It was as he was passing a tall building, its dark windows showing that it was commercial, that Bart called for a sudden stop.

'Wait a minute! Let me take a look at that place!'

The brakes squeaked as the driver pulled on the reins. Bart leaned out of his seat alongside the driver and surveyed the tall, gloomy building intently, its lower regions lighted by the reflected glow of the streetlamps.

'Caradoc-Wilson Railroad Corporation,' he murmured. 'That's what I wanted to see . . . OK, driver – take us back to the hotel.'

The driver nodded and started off again. Bart slowly relaxed in his seat, frowning hard to himself. Only when the hotel was reached did he seem to return to awareness, and after paying off the driver with a generous tip, he led the way into the lounge.

Meredith and Jane sat in armchairs on either side of Bart, and looked at him enquiringly. Bart fished a folded paper from his pocket.

'Take a look at this, Jane. I found it in the shirt of one of the gangsters last night.'

She unfolded the paper and studied it, then raised her eyes.

'Same kind of thing as you found on Don Saunders,

only maybe a little more detailed. The ranches are marked, but the ladder is there. I still don't see—'

'I think my son is working on the hypothesis that the shortest distance between two points is a straight line, Miss Jane,' Meredith commented, with his bland smile. 'The ladder is obviously meant to be a railway track, the rungs being sleepers.'

Bart stared. 'Who told you what I was thinking?'

'Nobody, son: I deduced it. The thought crossed my mind when I first saw the 'ladder'. When it cropped up the second time and I unintentionally made my remark about a straight line a process of reasoning went through my head – The map *could* be a plan of a potential railway, making a straight trip through Mountain Peak Valley between Wilson and Caradoc Cities. At the head of such a scheme would undoubtedly be a railroad company. You evidently had the same idea, and so came to this city – or were prepared to go on to Caradoc if need be – to find the head of the said railroad company. You did find it, in the building of the Caradoc-Wilson Railroad Company, where no doubt there lies part – if not all – of the answers to our troubles.'

Bart raised his hands helplessly in the air and let them fall back to his sides. His discomfiture was not alleviated by the explosion of Jane's laughter.

'And you kept it all a secret so you could steal a march on your father and do the thinking yourself! That's priceless!'

Meredith looked contrite. 'I didn't mean to steal your thunder, son. I merely followed out what seemed a natural sequence of reasoning and—'

'OK, OK,' Bart interrupted. 'I might have expected it. The only credit I can claim is that I did work it out in the same way without any help from you – for once. Now, let's get to the point. Do you think we're right, Jane?'

'I think so. You believe the Caradoc-Wilson Railroad Company want to pass a railroad straight through our valley, in order to cut out that huge detour and save travel time.'

'Yes, but not being over-scrupulous they don't want to pay the ranchers to get out and so they're driving them out by using paid thugs. Or perhaps they may have offered a price that hasn't been acceptable; or finally, the ranchers may have refused to go no matter what the price. Ranchers have a tendency to cling to their holdings. So, faced with this refusal to move, the railroad company is perhaps using arson and murder to blast the ranchers out of the way.'

'Definitely feasible, son,' Meredith said. 'The finding of two almost identical maps can hardly be coincidence – and then we have the added significance of the ranches being clearly marked on the second.'

'Meantime I'm still wondering who the mastermind is in the valley,' Bart mused. 'There must be a go-between. The railroad company could never handle it from two hundred miles away. Somebody in the valley is behind the terrorists, on the spot to give immediate orders . . . and the more I see of the evidence we've gathered the more I suspect Don Saunders. Don't forget that we found a similar map on him, as well as on one of the gang.'

'It looks that way,' Meredith agreed. 'Yet I cannot see why a man who has such influence and money should be willing to jeopardize everything by becoming the head of a gang of murderers. A pity we found no broken gun belt on his premises as further evidence.'

'We discussed that before and decided that perhaps Saunders is borrowing the belt from somebody else with the intention of deflecting suspicion to that person if things get too hot. The only way is to confront Saunders with what we know and try and make him talk. He's no liking for my judo grip!'

'That's one way,' Meredith said, 'but if the real mastermind is located in the headquarters of the Caradoc-Wilson railroad, there is the place to start.'

'Be mighty difficult without anything certain to go on,' Bart pointed out. 'We might try interviewing the head of the railroad, but a man like that would be hard to break down, and it would only put him on his guard for the future. But if we get the truth out of Saunders we know then what we're driving at. We can then take the authorities with us to question the head of the railway company and make him confess.'

Meredith pondered for a while and then motioned a waiter over to him.

'Tell me, my man, who is the most responsible person in the Caradoc-Wilson Railroad Corporation? And what kind of a man is he? I'm hoping to meet him.'

Convinced from the massive size and worldliness of the man addressing him that he was an important Eastern buyer, the waiter became low-voiced and confidential.

'The head man is Abel Grainger, sir. Between ourselves, he is somewhat autocratic. Comes here occasionally. Very dictatorial. Kind of gent you wouldn't like to cross. I s'pose he has reason to be that way, being the head of the Caradoc-Wilson Railroad.'

'Thank you.' Meredith slipped a tip into the man's hand and then raised his eyebrows questioningly at Bart and the girl. 'Apparently just the kind of man who would have his own way no matter how unscrupulous the method employed.'

'Like I said, we can't tackle a powerful man like that to his face,' Bart decided. 'He'd probably have us arrested for harassment. I'll get the truth out of Saunders first. We'll stay the night here and go back to Mountain Peak in the morning.'

9

ARRESTED FOR MURDER

It was early the following evening when the trio returned to the Slanting F to find Mike Farnon waiting anxiously to discover the outcome of their trip. Over the meal that he hastily got together whilst the three freshened up after their journey, Bart made the facts clear to the last detail.

Farnon listened in grim silence, eating and drinking meanwhile, then he fell to studying the two sketches Bart handed to him.

'Seems little doubt about it,' he said at last. 'Don Saunders must be mixed up in this. The two maps kinda prove it.'

'Did you ever have a railroad agent call on you, sir?' Meredith enquired.

'Nope. But I've been thinkin' about that broken gun belt. It might belong to just about anybody.' Farnon handed the papers back. 'It's unlikely that Saunders would himself go on each raid to direct operations, though he might go on some of 'em. That belt could belong to the sort of foreman, workin' under Saunders' orders, who in turn gets 'em from this guy Abel Grainger back in Wilson City. I think you should search Saunders' office. When he's out for business he wears two gun belts; in the ordinary way, only one.'

'Which is the one I've seen and it's OK,' Bart said. 'Dad and I searched his office but found no sign of a second gun belt.'

'Then mebbe you didn't look far enough. Where'd you search, Mr Meredith?'

'Drawers, cupboards, hooks, the safe. Every likely place.'

'That's where you went wrong,' Farnon said, grinning. 'You should have looked in the *unlikely* place. I've been in Saunders' office many a time for a chat, and I've seen him reach a gun from the well in his roll-top desk – that space where you push your legs in. I reckon he has a gun belt hidden there, mebbe fastened across the well from hook to hook, so's he can reach for a gun in a hurry if need be.'

'Most ingenious,' Meredith commented. 'I never thought of looking in such a place. However, the oversight can be rectified.'

'And tonight,' Bart said grimly, rising from the table. 'We're going this moment, Dad, to take another look round that office.' He glanced out of the windows. 'It's dark enough now for us to get moving.'

'You'd better wait a while,' Farnon said quickly. 'Don is usually sorting out accounts in his office around now. You wouldn't stand a chance for at least an hour. Tell you what's better: Let one of my boys go over to the Painted Lady and take a look-around. Minute he sees Don down in the saloon he'll come back and tell us. Once Don *does* come into the saloon he'll stay until closin' time. That'll make things clear for you to act.'

'Good idea,' Bart agreed, and his father nodded absently, his thoughts apparently on something else. Farnon got up and left the room, to return shortly.

'That fixed it,' he said, and there was the sound of a rider leaving the yard. 'I've sent Steve Armstrong. Usually Steve goes home with the rest of the outfit at sundown, but he got delayed tonight with an injured steer. He'll look the landscape over for you.'

Bart nodded and rolled a cigarette. His father slumped in silence, his hands interlocked on his middle and his blank, moonlike face turned towards the darkening window. It was impossible to judge what was passing through his mind.

'If Don Saunders does turn out to be the go-between in this valley terrorism, I'll be surprised,' Jane remarked presently.

Her stepfather lighted the oil-lamps on the table and then looked at her sharply.

'Why surprised? You don't think that Don's a square shooter, do you? What about the map he had?'

'As a matter of fact I do think Don's OK,' the girl answered. 'Otherwise I'd never have tolerated his attentions as I did before I met Bart. He's tough, possessive, and a bit of a brute, maybe . . . but not crooked.'

'I entirely agree with you,' Meredith said, still gazing at the window.

'You're both wrong!' Farnon declared stubbornly, lighting a black cheroot and sitting down. 'I know Don Saunders better than you. You surely don't suppose he ever got to bein' top man in this region – lawless as it is – by bein' downright honest?'

'Not downright honest, perhaps,' Jane acknowledged, reflecting, 'but he'd never stoop to murder and the destruction of ranches.'

'That polecat,' Farnon snapped, 'would do anythin' for money!'

The time passed by, until, a little over an hour after he had departed, Steve Armstrong returned. He came into the living-room tugging off his Stetson.

'Don just came down into the saloon,' he announced. 'He locked his office door behind him, so I reckon he's all set to stay there for the rest of the night if you two gents want to try somethin'.'

'Thanks, we do,' Bart said, rising. 'Ready, Dad?'

'Ready,' Meredith responded. He got up and tightened the buckles on his crossover belts.

'You'd better stay here, Jane,' Bart said as the girl also made to rise. 'Could be dangerous. If I do find a gun belt there's going to be one big showdown. Expect us when you see us, and if there is any more raiding shoot first and ask questions afterwards.'

Bart kissed the girl gently, reached for his hat, and then strode out on to the porch. Meredith followed him, adjusting his Homburg. Within minutes they had taken their horses from the stable and were on their way down the trail to town.

On reaching the town Bart led his horse down a side turning between the ramshackle buildings not fifty yards from the lights of the Painted Lady.

'This'll do,' he said, dismounting in the shadows and fastening the reins to the side props of the nearest building. 'The rest we'll do on foot – and we'll have to do a spot of climbing to get to that office. You prepared for that, Dad?'

'I'll manage somehow. Be careful not to be seen.'

Hugging the shadows they moved out of the side turning and on to the boardwalk of the main street again. It was empty; at this hour everybody was either in the saloon or else at home.

The two men eventually reached the alley at the side of the saloon and stood contemplating the outside of the building in the reflection from the kerosene lights.

'That's his office window up there,' Bart said, pointing to it perched over the slanting roof that formed the top of the side boardwalk, going round the building. 'Get ready for a climb.'

For Bart the task was easy; but his father found it a different matter. He puffed and struggled and shoved, until at last Bart had hauled him over the edge of the roof gutter and on to the steep slope. Moving up it cautiously, they finally reached the locked window and Bart pulled at it gently.

'Just a simple catch across both sashes. This shouldn't take long.' He tugged out his penknife and slid the blade between the sashes. Pressure released the old-fashioned type catch and the rest was simple. Silently he slid into the dark, tobacco-fumed office beyond and Meredith followed him.

'I've brought a candle,' Meredith said, tugging it from his pocket, and lighting it with a match.

Bart half-smiled to himself at the prescience of his father as the small flame, shielded by Meredith's fingers from giving a direct glare detectable outside, cast a glimmer about the office. Bart went quickly to the door, pushed over the small bolt, and then returned to the roll-top desk. On their knees, he and his father looked inside the well in the centre. The light from the candle immediately revealed what they were looking for.

'Apparently Farnon was right,' murmured Meredith, and he lifted down the gun belt. In grim silence they crouched, looking at the broken end of the belt. The leather was dirty and chewed which betokened a rip of long standing.

Bart got to his feet. 'This would seem to settle it, Dad. Don Saunders is the man we want – and the murderer of Dave, or at least one of those responsible for bringing about his death.'

'So it would appear,' Meredith agreed. He seemed to be puzzling something out to himself, then he added, 'I assume you'll want to confront Saunders with the evidence?'

Bart hung the belt back in position and then straightened up again.

'I'm not going to show him the belt, but I *am* going to get the truth out of him; let him realize that I know he owns the belt. Then we'll see how he reacts with everyone in the saloon as witnesses.'

Meredith drew back the door bolt, and blew out the candle. He returned it to his pocket and headed for the window. He raised it and glanced back towards Bart. 'I take it we'll enter the saloon in the normal way by the front?'

'By the front,' Bart agreed. 'We don't want to put him on his guard by going down from this office.'

Silently they left by the way they had come in, sliding down the roof and returning to their horses. They walked the animals round to the front of the saloon, tied them to the hitch rail, and then strolled into the din and fumes of the Painted Lady.

They soon spotted Saunders in his usual managerial position by the pillar, from which he could survey the proceedings.

Hands on his gun butts Bart made his way amidst the tables, his father behind him. This time there was no sign of laughter; most of the habitues had learned by now that the dude and his Homburg-hatted father could be dangerous if it came to it. Don Saunders for his part smiled sardonically as he beheld the pair approaching him. He threw down his stub of cheroot and crushed it with his heel.

'You two again! Have a drink?'

'No,' Bart answered curtly. 'All I want with you, Saunders, are a few words.'

Saunders shrugged. 'Who am I supposed to have insulted this time?'

'What's your connection with the terrorists in this valley, Saunders?' Bart asked, keeping his voice low. 'You had a map of this district in your pocket, all set with a rail-road running through it. That map dropped out of your pocket when you and I settled our differences last time I was in here.'

'So that's what became of it?' Saunders reflected, shrugging. 'Yeah, sure it belonged to me, but that doesn't make me a triggerman. You're loco to think otherwise!'

'One of them was carrying a similar map, but much more detailed. That kind of coincidence is too obvious to be credited. It might make you the head of the gang around these parts. I've tied up this terrorist set-up with one Abel Grainger over in Wilson City – and that ties up with a man in this valley who's running things for him. You, Saunders.'

'That's just plain crazy.'

'Is it? Then how do you explain a torn gun belt hidden in your desk-well? I happen to know that that belt was worn by one of the terrorists responsible for my brother's death. When I was last here looking for something, that was it.'

'Then why didn't you just say so? As for there bein' a torn gun belt in my office, and in the desk-well, you're plain nuts!'

'We've just seen the gun belt and returned it to its

hiding-place,' Meredith remarked, his eyes fixed intently on Saunders' face as though trying to analyse his expression.

Saunders leaned back against the pillar and frowned. 'I know nothing about any gun belt, or the terrorists,' he said. 'As for that map . . . Some time ago a guy came to me from the Caradoc-Wilson Corporation and he offered me ten thousand dollars for this saloon of mine, and another ten thousand for my ranch, cattle, and everythin' else . . .'

'Keep talking,' Bart said.

'Not bein' plumb crazy I turned him down. Both my ranch and saloon are worth a hell of a lot more than that! This guy said the Caradoc-Wilson Corporation was figurin' on drivin' a railroad straight through the valley, and my ranch and saloon were in they way. He explained where the railroad would come and I drew a sketch of it as he talked, to weigh up later to myself. I must have left it in my pocket, I suppose.'

'Sounds logical to me,' Meredith commented, and looked at Bart.

'Too logical!' Bart retorted. 'You've had plenty of time to think up that excuse since you knew you'd lost your plan—'

'That's the truth, you damned fool!' Saunders snapped, straightening up again.

'OK, let's forget the gun belt for a moment,' Bart said quietly. 'You must be aware that the murderous terrorism in this valley is all caused by the Caradoc-Wilson Railroad. There can't be any other explanation.'

'Sure I know it – so probably does the sheriff and other people. They don't do anythin' because they know they can't fight a combine as tough as the Railroad. They prefer to stick to tryin' to dry-gulch the actual terrorists themselves if the chance arises. As for me, I ain't bothered.

I'm quick enough on the draw to look after my own interests.'

'I don't believe it!' Bart retorted, whipping out his right-hand gun and prodding it into Saunders' stomach. 'There simply isn't another man in this valley who'd be more likely to lead the terrorists than you! Admit it!'

He had deliberately raised his voice now. The words had floated to the men and women at the nearest tables. As they turned and saw the revolver levelled at Saunders they began to rise, forming a circle. The memory of the last struggle in which Bart and Saunders had been involved had not yet died.

'Stop talkin' like a blasted idiot!' Saunders snapped, as the men and women gathered about and behind him.

Saunders suddenly lunged forward, his hand blurring down to his gun. Automatically Bart fired, hardly realizing that he had done so. With the fumes of cordite drifting round his nostrils he watched Saunders slowly crumple; then fall heavily to the floor and become still.

Meredith looked down at the body impassively, but his blue eyes had a curious glint in them as he studied one particular cowpuncher in the little gathering behind where Saunders had stood.

'*Make way there!*'

Sheriff Curtis pushed his way through the gathering. He dropped on one knee beside Saunders, examined him briefly, and then looked up.

'I was in here and heard the shot,' he said, grim-faced. 'And you're one damned fool, feller, to shoot like that in front of all these witnesses. You're under arrest for murder . . . Saunders is dead!'

Bart looked at his gun stupidly and then at the man sprawled on the floor.

'But – but he *can't* be!' he gasped. 'And if he is dead, it was self-defence! He tried to draw on me – anybody here will tell you that!'

One or two in the gathering murmured an assent, whilst others remained silent. Then Meredith broke in emphatically:

'It was self-defence, Sheriff. If my son had not—'

'Self-defence or murder – the trial can figure that one out. Right now, Bart Meredith, I'm holding you for murder. Give me your guns.'

Bart slowly held out the one in his hand and then gave the sheriff its twin.

'You ought to know, Sheriff, this man's death has done this valley a service. He was the go-between for the terrorists and the railroad corporation who are trying to clear the ranchers out of the district.'

Curtis eyed him sourly. 'So you've got on to the fact that the railroad corporation is back of the terrorism, huh? We realized that long ago, but findin' proof is a different matter. Otherwise we'd have had the authorities on the job long ago. It's only a theory at best – and without proof we're corralled.'

'I've got proof in a gun belt up in Saunders' office,' Bart insisted. 'The leader of the band who strung up my brother and fired his ranch was wearing that belt. I saw it – and so did my father here.'

'Right enough,' Meredith confirmed.

Sheriff Curtis shrugged. 'Darned flimsy evidence, I reckon – and where's the point in provin' anything against a dead man? Doesn't show his connection with the railroad corporation, does it?'

'Perhaps not,' Bart responded, 'but there could be information amongst Saunders' private papers which will prove it.'

'Mebbe.' The sheriff clearly wasn't convinced. 'We'll

take a look later, anyways, in readiness for the trial. In the meantime you're a-comin' with me . . . Let's go.'

Meredith returned to the Slanting F towards midnight, to find both Jane and her stepfather still up and anxiously awaiting news. When only Meredith entered the living-room they stared at him, then at one another.

'Bart's in jail,' Meredith explained – then as he saw the girl change colour he raised a hand gently. 'Don't worry, Miss Jane. It's just a misunderstanding—'

'What in hell is he in jail for?' Farnon demanded.

'Murder, I'm afraid . . .' Meredith sat down wearily, passed a hand over his semi-bald head, and went on to outline the details. They were sufficient to get Farnon on his feet and pacing angrily up and down in the lamplight.

'Rubbish!' he declared. 'Your son ain't the kind of man to murder anybody – 'less it was in self-defence like you said. When I see Curtis I'll tell him what I think about him!'

'I'm sure you will,' Meredith said, 'but I don't think it will help. Curtis is only doing his duty as sheriff—'

'But just look at the facts,' Farnon insisted doggedly. 'You found that gun belt at last, in Saunders' own office. What more proof could there be than that that he's the man back of the raids in this valley? Shootin' a man like him is a public service, and I'll tell Curtis so first thing tomorrow.'

'But how can we help Bart?' Jane asked anxiously. 'With all those witnesses present who saw him shoot Don, he's going to have a terrible time trying to prove it was self-defence. Everyone knows about that terrific fight they had! And don't you see that the information about the gun belt only gives Bart a *motive* for wishing to kill Don – because he was the man responsible for killing his brother! It's a horrible business – what can we *do*, Mr Meredith?'

Instead of answering directly, Meredith asked a question.

'You said that you trusted Don Saunders? That for all his personal faults you didn't think he was crooked?'

The girl nodded. 'I actually quite liked him until Bart came along.'

'I see . . . Thank you, Miss Jane.' Meredith heaved to his feet. 'If anybody is to get my son out of his predicament that person will be me – and first thing tomorrow I shall set about that task. And what's more, I'll do it!'

'If only you can . . .' Jane gazed up into his moonlike face. 'But what can you do?'

'Plenty, believe me!' Meredith's benign smile gave nothing away. 'Just leave everything to me. In my years of being a successful businessman I have cultivated the habit of keeping my eyes and ears very wide open and my lips shut. Tonight I saw something that I believe will help release my son – and, even, clean up the gang of terrorists haunting this valley . . . Meantime, it's late,' he concluded. 'I'll just have to sleep on it. I bid you both goodnight.'

The girl and her stepfather murmured something in response and Meredith went majestically from the room.

Whilst he was slowly undressing in the light of the oil-lamp he went over a variety of points in his mind and finally smiled at his reflection in the dressing-table mirror.

If – as seems certain – Saunders was not the terrorist leader, then only one other person can be. Ingenious, but as far as I am concerned, not quite ingenious enough . . .

10

POWER OF SUGGESTION

Immediately after breakfast the following morning Meredith, Jane and her stepfather set off for town. It was towards 9.30 when Farnon drew up the buckboard and team outside the sheriff's office. Curtis watched the trio enter as he sat at his desk in the corner by the window

'Howdy, folks,' he greeted, rising. 'This a deputation?'

'You can call it that,' Farnon responded. 'What the blue hell d'you mean by arrestin' young Bart Meredith for murder? If he shot Don Saunders it was his good deed for the day, whether it was self-defence or not!'

'Naturally you'd think that, Mike,' Curtis answered drily. 'Amongst Saunders' papers, which we went through last night, was a little item referring to you. I reckon you owed him some eight thousand dollars, didn't you?'

Jane gave a start and looked at her stepfather. Mike Farnon straightened up and shrugged.

'Yeah, I guess I did, though I figure you sayin' it out loud like that is kind of indiscreet.'

'I don't aim to be discreet,' Curtis said stolidly. 'You

owed him that, and now you don't have to pay it. No wonder you ain't beefin' about Saunders bein' shot dead!'

'This true, Dad?' Jane asked quietly, catching his arm. '*Did* you owe him all that money?'

'Yeah. I just gambled a bit more than I should have – but I was all set to pay it back. There's nothin' in it that need worry you.' Farnon turned back to the sheriff. 'Just the same, Curtis, Bart Meredith ain't a killer, and you know it!'

'Saunders was shot dead and he fired the gun.' Curtis said implacably. 'The bullet was removed and checks with his weapon. His guilt is for the jury to decide – not me.'

'Anything to stop me having a word with Bart, Mr Curtis?' Jane asked.

'You can't go into his cell, but I guess you can talk to him through the bars. Through that first door there.'

As the girl turned quickly and went out, the sheriff looked questioningly at Meredith. Bart's father cleared his throat gently.

'My reason for being here, Sheriff, is to make one or two enquiries on my own account. If you've been through Mr Saunders' effects you must have found that torn gun belt?'

'Yeah – we found it. Also another gun belt in a panel behind the wall.' The sheriff paused as he rolled himself a cigarette deftly. 'I can't quite figure out that torn gun belt. I've known Saunders for years and never saw him wearin' that torn belt. But I often saw him with the other one. He used it sometimes when he was "on business" so to speak – like formin' part of a posse, mebbe.'

'Which suggests that the torn gun belt was planted there to deflect suspicion on to him,' Meredith commented.

'Could be,' the sheriff said, and lighted his cigarette.

132

'You're wrong,' Farnon argued. 'I know Saunders had that gun belt hidden in the desk-well because on two occasions I saw him snatch a gun from there – mostly when I talked a bit too free for his likin',' he added, with a leathery grin.

'I assume,' Meredith continued, 'that there'll be an inquest?'

'This mornin'. The verdict will likely be murder – and I reckon that young feller's only hope is to plead self-defence when his trial comes up in about a fortnight. I've got him a good lawyer to defend him – Gerry Bassington, down the high street here.'

'Tell me,' Meredith said, 'did you find any evidence connecting Saunders with the Caradoc-Wilson Corporation?'

'Not a sign. Guess that was just some crazy bee your son got into his bonnet.'

'Thank you,' Meredith said. 'Now might I have a word with my son?'

'Sure – but I'd ask you to leave your guns with me whilst you do it. Same door as the gal took.'

Meredith complied, moved to the door and then waddled down the short length of stone passage until he came into the drab area of the little lean-to jail at the back of the sheriff's office.

'Find out anything, Mr Meredith?' Jane asked anxiously, turning from the barred door of Bart's cell.

'No more than I expected,' he replied ambiguously. Then beaming on Bart between the bars of the cell door he added, 'Good morning, son. Things are looking a bit tricky, aren't they?'

Bart turned an unshaven and grim face.

'Hell of a lot worse than that, Dad,' he said bitterly. 'I did shoot Saunders – and from the reaction of the folks in the saloon last night I don't think many of them will speak up for me. They don't like me – or you. We're outsiders. I've just been talking things over with Jane, and between us we can't think of anything to help my case.'

'But *I* can, son. The shooting of Saunders was a rather ingenious manoeuvre,' Meredith said. 'As a bystander, I saw it all happen.'

'*Manoeuvre?*' Bart frowned. 'How could it be? Saunders suddenly came forward, his hand dropping to his gun – so I had to shoot first.'

'That's just how it *looked*, son. Whilst you were talking to Saunders – with the gun pointed at his middle – an ugly-looking puncher was standing right behind him – a person I would instantly recognize again. He deliberately *pushed* Saunders forward: I saw it happen. In this part of the world, a man's first instinct is to drop his hand to his gun, and that is what Saunders did. You misinterpreted his forward movement and gun-hand action – as it was intended you should – and fired to save yourself. The shot was fatal. Somebody is a psychologist. Somebody knew that Saunders would drop his hand to his gun if pushed suddenly forward – and that you, not being very experienced, would fire to save yourself. The trick worked, diabolically well in that you find yourself facing a murder charge – and maybe a hanging too. So far the trick has succeeded . . . but only so far. Incidentally, I don't want either of you to mention what I saw – until I tell you otherwise. There's a reason.'

'So that was it,' Bart breathed, a gleam in his eyes. 'But would that ugly puncher have had the brains to think of a scheme like that?'

'No, son. He just acted under orders.'

'But whose orders? The sheriff told me that there's no evidence been found to link Saunders with the Wilson-

Caradoc Railroad and the terrorists. The story he told us about the plan might have been true . . .'

'It was, son. I'm sure of it now.'

'In which case . . . Look here, Dad,' Bart broke off, 'didn't it strike you as odd that the sheriff was so conveniently handy in the saloon when I fired that fatal shot?'

'Not really. The saloon is the spot where most of the denizens of this town collect in their off time, and it's his job to watch them.'

'But doesn't it seem odd,' Bart insisted, 'that, knowing as he does that the railroad corporation is responsible for the trouble around these parts, the sheriff doesn't do something more about it? He just seems to be pinning his hopes on the chance of catching the actual terrorists. And when have we seen him or his deputies on the look-out for them?'

'So you think, son, that the sheriff may be mixed up in it somewhere?'

'It's possible, isn't it? On the night Dave was murdered he was pretty glib about the whole thing, saying that it was useless to try and catch the gangsters.'

'In a way, though, it *is* a difficult job to catch the gangsters,' Jane said pensively. 'And if Mr Curtis is mixed up in things, he seems to have taken care of you as a potential source of danger, but left out your father as not worth bothering about – with all respect to you, Mr Meredith.'

'No offence taken, Miss Jane. I like people to think I am somewhat vague and pompous: makes things easier for me to spring a surprise when I'm so minded... However, whilst we are considering this new angle of Sheriff Curtis, we still need to consider the matter of the torn gun belt. How did it get into Saunders' office?'

At that moment there came an interruption as the sheriff himself appeared in the passageway, Farnon hovering behind him.

'Time's up for talking,' he announced. 'I've got an inquest to hold on Saunders and my prisoner's got to be taken along to the Painted Lady, where we're holdin' it. You'll have to be there, Mr Meredith, as a witness.'

'Dad and I will be there too,' Jane said quickly.

'But not as witnesses.' The sheriff drew his gun and then opened the cell door. 'OK, feller, start movin'. Just go where I tell you.'

Bart obeyed and the journey led him along the board-walk to the nearby Painted Lady. Jane and her stepfather followed in the rear of the sheriff and Meredith came up behind, his round face expressionless as he reholstered his guns which Curtis had returned to him once they were outside.

Inside the saloon, roughly arranged to resemble a court, there was a fair gathering of the town's inhabitants. Sheriff Curtis, as chairman of the proceedings, fired all manner of questions. This was not so much a trial as an inquiry into the cause of death.

Meredith gave his evidence – but he deliberately did not mention the pushing incident, simply reaffirming his belief that it had been a case of self-defence. Thereafter he seemed to relapse into something approaching slumber for the rest of the hearing. He opened his eyes again when the jury, convened on the spur of the moment, was of opinion that murder had been done.

'Which means, Bart Meredith, that you go back to jail to await trial in two weeks,' Curtis said grimly. 'In the meantime, any of you who want to give Saunders a decent funeral can do so. If none of you wants to it will be up to the mayor to arrange a civic one at the town's expense. The inquiry is finished.'

Amidst the stir and bustle of men and women Meredith stood motionless, until he caught sight of Jane and her stepfather as they came past him.

'If you should see Bart tell him to remain confident,' he instructed the girl, catching her arm. 'I'm going into action now to clear him. I'll return to the Slanting F later.'

'For heaven's sake succeed!' Jane breathed; then she went on her way.

Meredith watched her go, joining her stepfather amidst the throng heading for the batwings, then he moved in the opposite direction towards the back of the crowd. Ever since the inquiry had opened he had kept his attention fixed on one particular member amongst the spectators – the close-eyed, big-mouthed cowpuncher whom he had seen perform the 'stunt' the previous evening. Now Meredith glided in his wake and followed him out on to the boardwalk. Gently Meredith withdrew his gun and placed the muzzle in the small of the man's back.

'Keep moving,' he murmured. 'I want a word with you.'

'Huh?' The man swung round, glaring.

'Do as I say. I'm holding a gun in your back.'

The man looked about him frantically, but he and Meredith were alone on the boardwalk. The people had filed into the street and were going their different ways in a haze of dust.

'Take me to where you live,' Meredith ordered abruptly.

'I'll be durned if I—'

The gun jabbed viciously.

The puncher motioned. 'I've a shack at the end of the street.'

'We'll go to it. Walk naturally. One false move and it's your last.'

Seeing no way of escaping from his predicament, the puncher led the way to a broken-down dwelling that was little better than a glorified shack.

'Your stables, or your home?' Meredith enquired, contemplating it in disgust.

'It's where I live, blast yuh! Most of the time I'm workin' at a ranch out on the north trail.'

'All right, we'll talk inside.'

The puncher opened the rickety front door of the place and walked into a single sparsely furnished and untidy room. On the rough table stood an unwashed plate, a coffee jug, half a loaf of bread, and some butter. In one corner was a dully glowing heater-cooker with a funnel-like chimney. Meredith glanced around him briefly, his gaze taking in the open doorway leading to another room – presumably a bedroom – and then his attention came back to the grim-faced puncher.

'Sit down,' Meredith ordered, nodding to the solitary chair at the table. The man did so nervously. He was finding it difficult to assess just how far this enormous man with the calm voice, expressionless face, and steady revolver would go.

'You are going to give me some information, my friend.' Meredith half-perched on the table and laid his punctured Homburg down gently beside him.

'About what?' the puncher's voice was truculent, but with a hint of fear.

'Last night you deliberately pushed Don Saunders so that my son was tricked into shooting him.'

'*I* pushed him? You're crazy, Homburg! That dude shot him fair and square. Everybody saw it.'

'I can see,' Meredith sighed, getting up again, 'that you are going to be troublesome. So be it.'

Keeping the man covered, he backed across to the door, bolted it, and then came to the table. Unfastening one of his gun belts he went down on his knees and with one hand buckled the man's feet to the chair. The puncher resisted, until the gun pointed straight at his heart; then he became passive. With the man's own gun belt, the weapon from which he tossed over his shoulder, Meredith strapped the man's arms to his sides.

'What the hell good will this do you, Homburg?'

'We'll see,' Meredith answered calmly; then loosening his neckerchief he tied it tightly over the man's eyes. This done he laid his gun handy on the table for instant use and removed a large jackknife from his pocket, snapping back the largest knife blade.

'Now what you doin'?' the puncher shouted hoarsely, catching the sound.

Meredith didn't answer. Instead he looked inside the metal coffee jug and then placed it silently inside the dully glowing coke-heater so that it would warm up rapidly. He returned to the table and again half-perched on the edge.

'My friend, I'm giving you the choice of telling me the truth – or dying! I once studied surgery,' Meredith continued, and did not even blink at his colossal fabrication. 'I know just where every important nerve and artery of the human body is situated. If you are prepared to talk I shall do you no further harm, apart from handing you over to the sheriff. If you remain obstinate, I intend to slit an artery in your arm, and it will continue to bleed steadily – and fatally – until you speak. When you speak I can arrest the flow. If you remain silent you will die. It's up to you!'

The cowpuncher struggled savagely, before falling back limply, unable to break free. Meredith went over to the stove, and still without a sound he removed the coffee pot. Holding it with his handkerchief he brought it to the table and set it down. He raised the lid and considered the steaming liquid.

'Well?' he snapped harshly.

'Do what the hell y'like!' the puncher retorted. 'I ain't talkin'!'

'Not only will you admit that you pushed Saunders last night,' Meredith continued, 'but you will also tell me from whom you received your orders.'

The puncher remained stubbornly silent.

'As you wish.' With the blade of the knife Meredith ripped open the man's shirtsleeve just above the point where the strap pinned him. He reached out to the coffee pot, dipped his finger in the liquid to test its temperature, and then he brought the sharp tip of the blade deliberately down the man's arm. The puncher winced and shoved violently, trying to tug his arm free of the strap – and failing. Meredith raised the coffee jug and holding it steady he allowed a gentle stream of warm coffee to course down the man's arm.

'I have slit a vital artery, my friend,' Meredith explained. 'I can tourniquet it and stop the bleeding when you wish to speak. Until then you will have the pleasure of finding yourself becoming gradually weaker from loss of blood.'

'You dirty bastard!' the blindfolded puncher shrieked, heaving so violently that the chair rocked. 'What've you done to me?'

Meredith slightly increased the flow of warm coffee.

'For God's sake, what've you done to me?' the man shrieked, as he began to feel the coffee soaking into his pants on the chair.

'Did you or did you not push Saunders last night?'

'I – I—' The man was beginning to gasp in real panic. 'You'll stop this – this blood flowin' if I talk?'

'Only if you tell me the truth.'

'OK, OK – you win. Stop it! *Stop it!* I shoved him. I was told to. It was to make the dude shoot at him.'

'Good! And who gave you those orders?'

'They came first from Abel Grainger of the railroad – *stop the blood! Stop it!*

'Not until you tell me who is running things in this valley!'

'I – I—' The puncher's breathing rasped suddenly and he became silent, his head falling forward slightly. Meredith frowned, suspecting a trick, then as the man remained motionless he slowly put down the coffee jug and felt at the puncher's wrist.

There was no pulse.

Meredith blinked slightly. 'Dead!' he muttered. 'Dead from the sheer fear of something that never happened! Just the power of suggestion – warm coffee, a scratch down the arm, and a few well-chosen words. And these Westerners are supposed to be tough!'

He removed the belts, returning one belt to the man's waist and buckling his own into place. Then he dried the coffee with a rag and threw it in the coke-stove.

Heart failure, he thought to himself. Nothing else but – which lets me out, but without him telling me who the leader of the terrorists is in this valley. Though I think I know that already – and at least I have confirmed that Abel Grainger is back of everything. That takes thinking about . . .

He put on his hat and left the shack, closing the door gently; then he glanced up and down to be sure that nobody was passing. Laboriously he climbed the low fence at the rear, which eventually brought him back to the main street. From here he walked to the railroad station and from the solitary individual who ran the place purchased a return ticket to Wilson City.

'Reckon you're just plain lucky,' the stationmaster said, peering at him. 'Next train'll be here in ten minutes.'

*

Once he'd arrived in Wilson City later that evening
Meredith made enquiries at the station, which eventually
led him to a late-opening general stores with an outfitting
department.

Half an hour later, he was checking into the Pineview
Hotel, his appearance completely transformed. He was
wearing an immaculate suit of French grey – nor did the
shoulder-holster show much of a bulge – matched by a
very broad-brimmed grey trilby with a deep black band. A
stock tie with an unobtrusive stickpin and a white-silk shirt
with a trace of cuff revealed completed the effect. The new
suitcase he carried contained his former clothes. He now
appeared to be a man apparently possessed of extraordinary influence and purpose.

The clerk at the reception desk regarded him in some
doubt, obviously trying to remember where he had seen
the moonlike face, if not the magnificent attire, before.
His doubts vanished when Meredith informed him that he
had arrived for a business meeting with Abel Grainger the
following morning. The clerk immediately became obse-
quious. He turned to the key-rack and then swung round
the register.

'Room 105, sir. Boy! Take this gentleman's luggage up
to 105.'

Meredith signed 'Hiram J. Carruthers' with a flourish
and then followed the boy across the lounge. Once he was
alone in his room he smiled to himself and threw himself
on the bed. Lighting a cigarette he gave himself up to
thoughts – and more thoughts, all of them centred on the
interview he was going to have with Abel Grainger on the
morrow.

11

KILLER UNMASKED

With the same air of tremendous splendour Meredith entered the Caradoc-Wilson building at ten o'clock the following morning and paced gravely across the enormous entrance lounge.

When he came to the centre of the imitation marble flooring he paused and looked about him. He was thus engaged when a respectful voice spoke beside him:

'Can I be of service, sir?'

The speaker was a commissionaire, even larger than he was himself, looming beside him, resplendent in purple livery and brass buttons.

'Yes indeed,' Meredith assented. 'I am Hiram J. Carruthers, of Canadian Inter-Railways. I have an important matter to discuss with Mr Grainger personally. Since my being in this town is purely fortuitous, I was unable to advise him beforehand. Would it be possible to see him, please?'

The commissionaire looked as though he were trying to recall 'Canadian Inter-Railways', then with a salute he said he would make enquiry and went off to regions unknown. As Meredith waited, men and women came in and out of the building, some just the staff and others on business. They all regarded him curiously but respectfully, and went on their way.

'If you will come this way, sir?' the returning commissionaire murmured confidentially, and Meredith found himself escorted to the top floor. Passing along a softly carpeted corridor he had to go through three offices to reach the inner sanctum of Abel Grainger. First the general office, from where he was ushered to the general manager. From there he moved on to Grainger's personal secretary; and so finally into a large room overlooking the city, wherein Abel Grainger in person sat at a huge desk.

He rose as Meredith was shown in: a square-built immensely strong man with a thick neck and florid face. Money, overeating, and short temper all had their signatures upon him. But his manner was genial enough as he gripped Meredith's plump hand.

'Mighty glad to know you, sir,' he greeted. 'Always a pleasure to make the acquaintance of a man in the same line of business. Have a seat – and a cigar.'

Meredith had both, placed his trilby carefully on the end of the vast desk, and then beamed.

'I must apologize for not informing you in advance of my intention to call. However, since I am here I should explain that I represent, and am part-owner of, the Canadian Inter-Railways.'

'Can't say I've heard of them.' Grainger's small blue eyes narrowed. 'Naturally I know Canadian Pacific and—'

'As yet,' Meredith intervened smoothly, 'the Canadian Inter-Railways have not actually come into being. It is a top secret – hence my calling on you. Up to now I have been . . . hmm, prospecting.'

Grainger relaxed. 'I am all attention.'

'In general,' Meredith continued, 'the business is

bound up in British railway stock. It is intended to make large railroad extensions through Canadian territory. Dollar position, you understand,' he added vaguely, 'and in turn those extensions will eventually link up with the American railroad network.'

'Interesting,' Grainger commented. 'And where do I fit into this scheme?'

'I believe you own a considerable quantity of rolling-stock and railroad network in this particular district. The Caradoc-Wilson line?'

'The corporation does. I am the managing director.'

'Quite so. When the Canadian Inter-Railways scheme comes to fruition – as it inevitably will – we would like to take over certain portions of the Caradoc-Wilson line, for an agreed sum, of course, and have sole control of that particular portion.'

Grainger studied the inkwells in the mahogany frame on his desk.

'That, of course, would be entirely governed by what portions you would require. I'm not sure the board or the shareholders would be keen on the idea of selling out portions of our line. It is a singularly profitable concern.'

'With respect,' Meredith said, 'I feel inclined to challenge that statement.'

'Why?' Grainger snapped, his shortness of temper out of hand for a moment.

'On my journey to this city, I don't think I've ever seen such a roundabout track. You have nearly one hundred miles of surplus track. *That* can't be profitable!'

'It is profitable because there is no other road,' Grainger explained.

'Not yet there isn't,' Meredith smiled and carefully tapped cigar ash into a brass tray. Instantly Grainger became alert.

'Unless we can buy certain portions of your existing railroad and make it a joint affair between your company and the Canadian Inter-Railways,' Meredith continued, 'we shall build a direct line straight across country – a beeline across Arizona, in fact. A direct line between Wilson and Caradoc would be included, of course. I need not add that that might cause quite a lot of friction between your company and ours. Far better that your railroad be under joint control and, between us, we would cut the shortest possible route.'

Grainger was thinking swiftly, then:

'I don't think a joint ownership would be workable, Mr Carruthers. We already have our own plans for a direct route—'

'You have!' Meredith sat up in sudden interest. 'Have you perhaps some kind of plan, or sketch?'

'Well . . .' Grainger hesitated, then he shrugged. 'Yes, as a matter of fact I have. I can show you what I mean.'

'Good!' Meredith sat back in his chair, but his keen eyes never left Grainger as he crossed the office to a picture, pulled it aside on hinges, and then opened a wall-safe.

He fished about inside and then began to close the safe door again.

'I shouldn't,' Meredith stated crisply. 'Leave it open!'

Grainger twisted round in amazement. The barrel of Meredith's .38 was resting on the desk-edge, pointing steadily at the railroad man.

'What the devil—!' Grainger exploded, striding forward angrily; then he stopped and raised his hands as the gun barrel lifted menacingly.

'Sit down, sir,' Meredith ordered, getting to his feet. 'But keep yourself away from the desk itself. I'm taking no risk on secret buttons to summon help from your staff.'

As Grainger obeyed, his mouth set hard, Meredith

opened his case and took out a length of rope and with swift movements bound the railroad man's ankles to the chair, and his wrists to the chair-arms.

'Who the hell are you?' Grainger demanded, glaring. 'What's the idea?'

Meredith ignored him, went over to the door and bolted it, then picked up a neatly folded duster from the top of the filing-cabinet. He returned to Grainger, gagged him tightly and then smiled benignly.

'I came here only to look through your safe. Since I am not by profession a safe-breaker, I had to make you open the safe for me. I am not a railroad magnate, of course, and there is no such thing as Canadian Inter-Railways. I have been talking sheer gibberish to you!'

Grainger could only glare, his eyes bulging with fury as Meredith turned aside and went to the open safe, took out the papers and sorted them on the desk.

'Splendid!' Meredith murmured at length, holding up one particular sheet of foolscap. 'The very thing! A pay-roll statement of those involved in the raids on Mountain Peak Valley. I know all about the valley raids,' he explained, glancing down the pay-roll account as he spoke. 'On finding out that you are at the back of them – and planning on running your precious railway straight through the valley – I decided to tackle you first-hand. Surprising what a little culture in the voice and good clothes on the body can do, isn't it. Mmmm . . . I think I have everything here I need. Every name of those involved in the terror raids. It is going to make interesting reading for the authorities – particularly with the heading of the Caradoc-Wilson Corporation at the top of the paper!'

Meredith put the sheet carefully in his inside pocket, returned the unwanted material to the safe, then donned his hat, nodded, and went to the door. He unbolted it, stepped out and closed it behind him.

Minutes later he was in the hallway, where the commissionaire saluted him majestically.

'Everything all right, sir?'

'Simply splendid, my man,' Meredith agreed, handing him a tip. 'I have had a most remunerative interview, but I have to be going. Mr Grainger is somewhat tied up, you know.'

Meredith left the building quickly and returned to his hotel two blocks away. He wasted no time paying the bill and hiring a buckboard to whirl him to the station. He did not begin to breathe freely again until, in the train's lavatory, he changed back into his former attire, complete with Homburg, disposing of his immaculate clothes, garment by garment, in the desert alongside the railway track, throwing, last of all, the suitcase after them. The only thing he retained was the damning pay-roll evidence on the Caradoc-Wilson memorandum.

Well pleased with his day's work, he ate a good lunch and retired to the observation car to enjoy the afternoon sunlight and the scent of the desert and plain as the train pursued its rambling, roundabout course towards Mountain Peak.

For a while he had the fear that the train, by orders from headquarters, might at any moment be stopped and himself arrested for assault and robbery. If that happened he was ready to jump overboard – hence his being in the open observation car.

But nothing happened throughout the long, hot afternoon. Still fully prepared for trouble he alighted at the wayside halt of Mountain Peak at journey's end. The sun was not yet set even though its actual glare was masked by the mountains. There was no reception committee awaiting him. Mountain Peak had never looked more sleepy or dead.

He handed up his ticket to the grizzled emperor of the station.

'Anybody been enquiring about me?'

'How would I know?' the stationmaster replied. 'What's your proper name? I only know of yuh as "Homburg".'

'Randle Meredith.'

'Nope. Nobody askin' for anybody with a monicker like that!'

Meredith nodded and passed on his way into the main street, where he found the station wagon with the elderly driver half-nodding in the twilight.

'You have a passenger, my friend,' Meredith said, climbing up beside him. 'The Slanting F, if you please.'

'Yeah – OK.' The man stirred into life. 'No luggage, Homburg?'

'No luggage. And the name is Meredith.'

The driver grinned, whipped up the horses, and began the trip down the main street.

'Not a bad funeral they gave Don Saunders, was it,' he said as they hit the trail through the pastureland.

'Not being present, my friend, I am unable to say.'

Since Meredith passed no further comment the driver became silent, and in fifteen minutes he drew the wagon up outside the Slanting F, collected his fare, and departed in a cloud of dust.

Meredith walked majestically across the yard. Since screen and main doors were both propped open he walked into the ranch house to find Jane and her stepfather settling to the evening meal. The girl got quickly to her feet.

'Mr Meredith!' She caught his right hand eagerly as with his left he put down his hat. 'Where have you been?'

'Hang it all, gal, let the man get into the place,' Mike Farnon said, though his own eyes were darting enquiry.

'What have you found?' Jane persisted. 'With Bart facing that murder charge . . .'

'Perhaps,' Meredith said, 'it would be better if I told you everything over a meal, though I'm afraid I have nothing very important to relate.'

'That's a bit of a shock.' The girl released his hand slowly, her mood changing. 'I guess I'd better go and fix you up something to eat.'

'Thank you, Miss Jane.'

The girl went from the living-room and Meredith departed to his own quarters. Freshened up, he returned to the living-room table and settled down, passing a hand over his semi-bald head. Farnon looked at him curiously.

'Get far?' he asked, as they resumed the meal.

Meredith shrugged. 'Round and about. Since it seems to be common knowledge that the Caradoc-Wilson railroad is behind the terror in this valley I thought of tackling the head of the railroad, and went to Wilson City for that purpose. My interview was not much use, unfortunately. I realize, at last, that I do have limitations as a detective.'

'You mean you can't do anything more for Bart?' Jane asked sharply.

'Right now I just don't see how I can, and I just haven't the heart to tell him so personally.'

There was a long silence whilst Meredith ate slowly and Mike Farnon frowned hard at the table. Then he looked up to where the girl was sitting, gazing dumbly before her.

'Jane,' he said, 'I think you should go and tell Bart that things aren't workin' out as well as we'd figured. Break it to him gentle. Mr Meredith here was our last hope. Now he admits he's failed, I don't see where there's any use in Bart buoying himself up.'

'I'll do what I can,' Jane muttered, pushing aside her

plate and getting to her feet.

'It might be of assistance if I penned a few words myself,' Meredith added. He rose and went over to the writing bureau. 'Perhaps take off some of the strain. You can read the letter as you go, Miss Jane, then perhaps you'll have a better idea how best to break the news.'

The girl waited whilst Meredith wrote the note, then she took the unsealed envelope he handed her. He considered for a moment after she had gone, then returned to the table where Farnon, his own meal finished, sat brooding.

'I think, sir,' Meredith said at last, sitting back, 'it's time you and I came to an understanding.'

'About what?'

Meredith poured himself some coffee. 'My trip to Wilson City was not really so unfruitful. I didn't want Miss Jane to know. She's a decent, honest girl and the last thing I want to tell her is that her stepfather is the leader of this gang of valley murderers!'

Mike Farnon raised his right hand from below the level of the table-edge and the muzzle of his gun became visible.

'If this is intended to be a shock, Meredith, it ain't,' he said. 'I know that you saw Abel Grainger, bound and gagged him, and then escaped with a pay-roll sheet containin' the names of all the men in his employ, includin' the name of the valley leader. Naturally, my name would be at the top of the list.'

'Naturally, and Don Saunders was not even mentioned. Which makes you the man we're looking for.'

Farnon laughed shortly. 'The telegraph operator in town works for me secretly. Grainger uses it to send me emergency messages, which my man intercepts and passes to me. He told me all about a guy who answered your description, in a fancy outfit. We decided to wait and see if you'd the gall to come right back and bluff things out. You did – and that was your fatal mistake.' Moving forward, he yanked out Meredith's guns and threw them into a corner.

Unmoved, Meredith continued drinking his coffee.

'I've sent the gal away for only one reason,' Farnon continued. 'I love her, and I don't want her to ever find out that I'm the leader of the gang – the valley go-between. I'm goin' to burn this spread down, with you in it, and turn the cattle loose. When she gets back she'll think the terrorists have struck again and that you and me have perished in the flames. I'll be away by then, and I'll never come back. You've queered my game, Meredith, but you ain't got me. I'm too smart for you!'

'I wonder,' Meredith said, continuing with his meal. 'But first, perhaps you'd like to know how I first arrived at the conclusion that you were the man?'

Farnon shrugged. 'You can tell me if you like – before you die.'

'You were obviously the man Bart and I saw with the broken gun belt. Your voice was disguised, as no doubt it always is when on a raid – especially with the kerchief muffling it. Then Bart unwittingly told you what we knew about that gun belt.'

'Right,' Farnon agreed laconically. 'Luckily I wasn't wearin' it when you two guys turned up here with Jane. I'd sneaked in home by the back way and pretended to be asleep. Then Jane got up and went out. When the gun belt business came up I thought about destroying it – then I saw a way to pin the blame for everythin' on Don Saunders—'

'Yes, not least because you owed him eight thousand dollars. Your chance came when you sent a man in your employ to spy out the saloon for us. He took the broken gun belt and planted it in Saunders' office for us to find. No one else could have done it. From that moment onward I knew you were the man. But I needed proof. You knew my son, inspired by Jane, was getting difficult to handle, so with a double movement you planned to be rid of Saunders, or at least wound him severely, and get Bart arrested for injuring or killing him. Incidentally, I confirmed the truth from the puncher involved yesterday morning.'

'I was suspicious when I heard Lefty had died from so-called heart failure. So you were behind that.' Farnon laughed harshly. 'Well, that's kinda appropriate, I guess!' As Meredith looked his enquiry, Farnon added brutally: 'Lefty was the man who actually hanged your stubborn son – on my orders, of course.'

Meredith remained silent. It was impossible to read from his expression what he was thinking, but his eyes glinted dangerously. Farnon decided to twist the knife further.

'Want to know *why* I'm leadin' this terrorist gang? It was because I *wanted* to, and but for you I'd have blasted every infernal rancher out of this valley. I'd two reasons. One, to make money the easy way, by bein' paid for every raid by the Caradoc-Wilson Corporation, plus what I picked up from pillaged ranches. But most of all, to get my revenge! Years ago I was hounded out of this very valley for what was supposed to be cattle-stealin'. Later I proved my innocence and came back. But I never forgot that! Never! The chance to hit back came, and I used it. Most people accepted the fact that I was innocent of that cattle-stealin'. But one man who never believed it was Don Saunders, so I'd a special reason, apart from money, for gettin' him rubbed out. The other guy who kept bad mouthin' me and was a thorn in my side, was that damned son of yours.

So I saw to it that he got his come-uppance!'

Farnon waited for a reaction from Meredith but he disappointed. Instead Meredith asked another question:

'What about that affair of your stepdaughter being kidnapped? You must have arranged that too. You thought your men would kill me, and that Bart would go chasing after your stepdaughter, with you 'accidentally' finding where she was being held. It would then have been easy to pick off Bart and claim that the gangsters had done it.'

'That was the notion I had, but it didn't work out, thanks to your blubbery hide, and damned stratagems!' Farnon snapped. 'I tried again to bring you into the open by havin' my own spread attacked one night. I figured that if you were anywhere around you'd try a rescue – then you could both be taken care of without any suspicion attachin' to me. But you were *in the gang*, which was somethin' I'd never thought of. I admit that was a smart move.'

'Praise indeed,' Meredith murmured, his face impassive.

'Your latest moves weren't so smart,' Farnon sneered. 'With the evidence you have you could've gone straight to the sheriff with it instead of comin' back here and walking right into my trap.'

'Yes . . .' Meredith gave a sigh. 'I seem to have rather overplayed my hand. I came here because I wanted to keep my eye on you and make sure you didn't escape before I'd had a chance to hand over the evidence.'

'Speaking of evidence,' Farnon grinned cynically, 'I'll take that pay-roll sheet off you right now.'

Meredith put his hand in a pocket, but instead of the stolen document, he produced the makings and began to calmly roll himself a cigarette.

An ugly look came to the rancher's face and he waved his gun menacingly. 'I said give me that pay-roll sheet!'

'I heard you,' Meredith acknowledged. 'I haven't got it!'

'You're lyin'!' Farnon shouted. 'I know you didn't go to the sheriff first because I had a man hidden at the station, watchin' for you comin' off the train. He got here ahead of you and told me you were headed here on that old fool's station wagon.'

'I thought the place looked too deserted,' Meredith mused, lighting his cigarette.

Farnon wasted no further time on words. Still keeping his gun cocked he searched Meredith quickly with his free hand – with negative results.

'All right, where is it?' Farnon demanded. As Meredith continued to make no response he suddenly found his cigarette viciously slapped from his mouth. His hands were seized and securely fastened behind him to the chair. In the space of a few minutes, using a long length of lariat, Farnon had secured him immovably.

'I just remembered,' Farnon said. 'You went to your room to freshen up when you came back from your trip. You must have hidden the damned sheet there!' Farnon vented his anger by delivering a backhander to Meredith's face. He paused, breathing hard.

'I ain't got time to search for it. But it won't do you any good! When this place goes up in smoke – and you with it – that evidence will burn too, wherever it is. You can say hello to your son in hell, Meredith!'

Farnon turned aside and strode out of the room, the main door thudding to after him. Grim-faced, straining at his ropes, Meredith could hear Farnon moving about in the yard, then after a while there was the sound of a horse galloping away, followed by the unmistakable, acrid smell of burning.

Wisps of smoke began to come up through the cracks

in the floorboards, from where Farnon had evidently started a fire under the propped-up ranch. Its tinder-dryness from months of pitiless sunlight would make it an inferno impossible to extinguish once it gained a hold.

Struggling futilely against his bonds, Meredith was seized by a fit of coughing as thickening smoke belched suddenly. At the far end of the room there was a crackling spurt of flame from the floor. It leapt avidly to the walls, and the window curtains vanished in clouds of sparks. Perspiration wet on his face, Meredith suddenly keeled his chair over and tried desperately to roll towards the door-way, then stopped as flame suddenly burst through straight across his path. It looked like the end . . . .

Then there was a smashing of the window. Twisting his head, Meredith saw a revolver butt splintering the edges of glass away. A second or two later Bart vaulted into the room, hurtled across it, and slashed the imprisoning ropes with his jackknife. Without a word he helped his father up and they staggered blindly through the blazing hall and out into the clear sweetness of the evening air. Behind them a tower of smoke and sparks roared heavenwards. In the distance the cattle from the corrals were moving, stampeded by the holocaust.

'I thank God, and I thank you, son!' Meredith breathed, then he turned as Sheriff Curtis and Jane came forward.

'Where's Farnon?' Curtis snapped.

'He rode off,' Meredith told him.

The sheriff swung his horse round and began to investigate the area surrounding the blazing ranch. Jane came forward slowly, her face haggard.

'I could hardly believe it when I read that note you'd put in the unsealed envelope,' she said. 'About my stepfather being the gangster leader: but that pay-roll sheet you gave me to hand to the sheriff, inside the envelope, convinced me. I took it to him right away—'

'And he let me out on parole to help get Farnon, since there was no time to be lost getting a deputy,' Bart explained. 'Sorry, Jane, but your stepfather's got to be found and brought in. Damned smart of you, Dad, to send the information through Jane!'

'Just a last-minute inspiration when her stepfather sent her to see you. If Farnon can be located he can perhaps be forced into admitting that he made that puncher arrange the shooting of Saunders—'

'There he goes!' Curtis yelled suddenly, pointing through the smoke. 'He must have been hidin' in the orchard to see if the spread burned up properly.'

He spurred his horse forward towards a fast-fleeing rider, but at the identical moment ran into a dense westward drift of smoke. By the time he had broken free of it the horseman was no longer visible to him – but he was to Bart, standing clear of the smoke. He vaulted into his saddle, spurred the horse forward and hurtled in pursuit into the twilight.

Bart rode as he had never ridden in his life, knowing that once Farnon reached the mountains, instead of being the hunted, he would become the hunter, able to pick off his pursuers at will. Farnon turned in his saddle several times and fired, but the distance was too great and the target too uncertain for him to achieve his object.

Bart rode on savagely, until presently the mountain foothills came within view. Farnon turned again and fired, the bullet whanging close by Bart's ear. He spurred his horse to a final mighty effort and Farnon did likewise – too much so, for the twilight and loose rocks of the trail confused his mount and it stumbled, flinging him out of the saddle into the dust.

Without pause Bart hurtled on, jumped from his own saddle on the side furthest from Farnon and missed a bullet at the same instant. Farnon stumbled to his feet and levelled his gun for a second shot, taking his time as he saw that Bart had not drawn his weapons. Bart did not attempt to go for them; without breaking his stride, he bent, straightened, and hurled a rock instead. It hit Farnon clean on the forehead and his gun exploded harmlessly in the air as he stumbled backwards. Then Bart was upon him, pinning him down.

The same relentless judo grip that Bart had once used on Saunders descended and Farnon found himself nailed.

'OK, so you got me,' he panted. 'I ain't admittin' anythin' and the fire took care of the evidence . . .'

Bart did not answer. He was watching three riders emerging out of the twilight, resolving into Sheriff Curtis and Jane and Meredith.

The girl slid from the saddle and stared at her stepfather lying in the dust with Brad straddling him. Meredith alighted more slowly and was some little time before he caught up with Curtis and the girl.

'OK, Bart, you can let him up now,' Curtis said, his gun levelled. 'He's covered.'

'Before I let him to his feet,' Bart said, 'I want some information. In that letter you gave to Jane, Dad, you said you had positive evidence that I was framed for the murder of Saunders.'

'I had,' Meredith conceded. 'Unfortunately the puncher concerned died of heart failure and can't repeat what he told me.'

'But *you* can, Farnon,' Bart muttered, still pinning him down. 'Better start talking, or by God I'll—'

'All right, I'll talk. Just let me up!'

Bart released his hold and the rancher slowly staggered

upright, his tall frame seemingly relaxed in complete resignation.

'Yes, it was arranged,' he admitted. 'Lefty, the man Meredith tackled, was tipped off by my foreman – who supposedly went to spy out the land in the saloon – to do what he did. I figured it might cause you to shoot – and you did. But just the same—'

With a sudden swift movement Farnon whirled round. With a hammer blow he sent Sheriff Curtis stumbling backwards and at the same moment tore his gun out of his hand and levelled it. The others froze, the tables turned.

'I'm sorry you had to know all about this, Jane,' Farnon said bitterly. 'I had my reasons, and I reckon you'll discover them if you ask Meredith: I've told him everythin'. I've nothin' against you, gal, and never shall have . . .'

Farnon backed a few paces to where the horses were standing. Motionless, the group watched him, Curtis crouched on one knee, his face grim at the prospect of his quarry sliding away from him.

As he reached the nearest horse, Farnon put his foot in the stirrup, but instead of him vaulting upwards the saddle whirled round and deposited him with a crash in the dust. Immediately Curtis and Meredith were upon him.

'You'll spring no more tricks,' the sheriff snapped, picking up his gun and hauling the rancher to his feet. 'But what in hell happened to that saddle?'

'That was my doing,' Meredith smiled. 'I knew that if by some chance Farnon did manage to get the better of us he would immediately make for one of the horses, so I loosened all the saddles in readiness when we arrived here. You will recall that I delayed before joining you.'

'I'll be dad-blamed!' Curtis exclaimed, staring. 'I guess

you think of everythin', don't you?'

'I try to. Now perhaps I had better fix the saddles so we can get back to town. I assume, Sheriff, that you'll notify the authorities in Wilson City to pick up Grainger and then go after the rest of the gang in the mountains? Without a leader and paymaster they may not give much trouble . . .'

'You bet – and I'm takin' you along with me. You're a useful guy to have around.'

Meredith raised and lowered his Homburg gracefully and then set about the task of readjusting the saddles. Jane stood watching, Bart's arm about her shoulder. Her eyes strayed at last from her slumped, cornered stepfather to Bart's face in the twilight.

'Sorry it had to work out this way, Jane,' he murmured. 'But I did do my share towards nailing the gangsters, even if my father did most of it. And that means I've a question to ask you again . . .'

'It's answered,' the girl said quietly. 'And it's "yes"!'